tony parsons
on life, death
and breakfast

tony parsons
on life, death
and breakfast

HarperCollins*Publishers*

HarperCollins*Publishers*
77–85 Fulham Palace Road,
London W6 8JB

www.harpercollins.co.uk

Published by HarperCollins*Publishers* 2010
1

A catalogue record for this book
is available from the British Library

ISBN: 978 0 00 732785 0

Typeset in Futura Book by Palimpsest Book Production Limited,

FSC is a non-profit international organisation established
to promote the responsible management of the world's forests.
Products carrying the FSC label are independently certified
to assure consumers that they come from forests that are managed
to meet the social, economic and ecological needs
of present and future generations.

Find out more about HarperCollins and the environment at
www.harpercollins.co.uk/green

For Dylan Jones
From the Roxy to eternity

Introduction   1
 1 The Mid-Life Myth   9
 2 When Yobs Swear   17
 3 Dying Parents   27
 4 Angry Old Man   37
 5 Fear of Fake Breasts   45
 6 Humiliation   55
 7 Tough Guys Get Facials   65
 8 You Only Wed Twice   81
 9 Getting Tested   89
10 A Complicated Young God   99
11 The Gunfire Next Door   111
12 Performance Anxiety   119
13 Love Handles, Actually   127
14 Man and Boy Racer   137
15 Junk Sex   147
16 Tough Girls   155
17 A Bigger Cock Than That   163
18 Faulty Modern Men   171
19 Get Fit with Fred   181
20 Gentlemen, Please   191
21 How to Be Happy   199

22 *New Man, Old Lad*   207

23 *Fever Bitch*   215

24 *Double Standards Now*   225

25 *Fake Breasts Don't Bounce Back*   235

26 *The Secret of My Failure*   245

27 *Why Men Stray, Why Men Stay*   253

28 *The Formerly Young*   263

29 *Big World, Small Society*   273

Introduction

When I was a washed-up music journalist, wondering what to do with the rest of my twenties, not to mention my life, the telephone rang.

It was a friend on a women's magazine. She wanted to know if I would write something for them. One thousand words on 'Commitment'. The man's view. Sure, I said, before she had a chance to change her mind. I was desperate for work, and the red bills were piling up.

And that phone call saved my life.

Because when I sat down to write about commitment for my mate on the women's magazine, I discovered my subject.

Sex. Romance. Fathers. Sons. Men and women – especially that – how we struggle to find love, and what we do with it when we find it.

The great game that never ends.

My subject had been music, but that had gone by the time I was twenty-five. The musicians I had known, and loved, and written about, had all moved on. Some of them were trying to crack America. Some of them were dead. Some of them were trying to hold on to their sanity. But nobody was where they had been any more.

I had joined the *NME* at twenty-two and it was what I did

instead of university or National Service. I went in as a boy and I emerged as a man. Or, if not exactly a man, then at least a boy who had taken lots of drugs and met Debbie Harry. But it was never meant to last forever, and it didn't. By twenty-five I was out of a job, and penniless, and a father. By twenty-nine I was out of a job, and out of a marriage, and penniless, and a single dad.

So whatever way you looked at it, things were definitely going downhill.

I had dropped out of school at sixteen with wild, impractical dreams of being a writer. After years of low-paid jobs that ended with the night shift at Gordon's gin distillery, I landed that job on the *NME*. They hired me because I had published a novel called *The Kids* – exactly the kind of callow, feverish rubbish that usually remains mercifully locked in some teenager's bottom drawer – and, far more importantly, I looked quite good in a cheap leather jacket.

I was a writer at last. But in the music press, the only vocational training I ever received focused on teaching me about taking drugs with rock stars. How to pass a joint to Bob Marley. The correct etiquette at a Keith Richards' heroin bust. How to offer Johnny Rotten some of your amphetamine sulphate without making some dreadful *faux-pas*. When I was on the *NME*, the creative writing thing was far less important than being able to hang out with Iggy Pop all night. I really wanted to write – it was the only thing I had ever found that I was halfway good at – but after leaving the *NME*, I found I had lost my subject without even really serving my apprenticeship.

Until I got that phone call.

So I wrote my little piece on commitment. And then I started to get other phone calls. The same sort of thing. And I realised that I loved it. Writing about the great game. Men. Women. Family. Fathers and sons. Husbands and wives. Sex and romance and what happens when you can't tell the difference. And the happy days when there really is no difference. How we feel when it all comes apart, and how we never stop hoping that we will get just one more chance to get it right. Becoming a parent and watching your own parents age and die. Finding love and then misplacing it somewhere, or having it snatched away from you.

The money wasn't terrific, but it was a living, just about – and I hadn't been making a living for a long time.

Money had not been important when I was at the *NME*. After a night of rock and roll decadence, me and Julie Burchill – then my girlfriend, later my wife, and a bit later still my ex-wife – would often take R. Whites lemonade bottles back to the local shop, collect our tube fare, and go to work, giggling like a pair of happy urchins who were exactly where they wanted to be. We didn't need money. Apart from the deposits we claimed on lemonade bottles to pay our tube fares.

But then I became a grown-up – with a wife, and a baby, and a divorce, and a broken heart, and a broken boiler, and bills that I could not pay. And money would matter from now on because I could never again pay my way in the world by taking back a few R. Whites lemonade bottles.

Don't you hate it when that happens?

I could have made the music thing last a few more years. I was still young. I still had my leather jacket. Ian Dury wanted me to go on the road in America, and Madness seemed like nice boys – but what would have been the point? I would have been faking it. The bands that I had really loved were elsewhere – on *Top of the Pops* or fighting heroin addiction or recording their difficult second albums in New York. Staying up for three days and nights in a row loses its appeal after a while. And I had a little son. And going to America with a band could never have been the same again.

What I remember most about my days on the *NME* was going to the Speakeasy with an unknown, unsigned young band called The Clash . . . and being turned away because we were not sufficiently cool. Not them. Not me. Not even the whole job lot could scrape together the cool quotient required to get us into the Speakeasy. Somehow I cherished that memory above the others. But those days were gone. And with them went my career.

That phone call from my friend on the women's magazine gave me back my career. It was the mid-eighties, and a great time for magazines, and for newspapers. Looking back, they seem like the last of the boom years. With the Internet still some years away, there was suddenly all this space to fill. And although my early gigs were all on women's magazines, or on the women's pages of national newspapers, soon there were all these magazines for men that were not simply about fishing, or football, or the new Ford Mondeo.

After the storming success of *The Face*, my old *NME* editor Nick Logan started *Arena*, the first British magazine for men, and that opened the gates for *Esquire, Loaded, FHM, Nuts* and British *GQ* – where many of the articles included here come from.

It gave me more than a living. It gave me confidence. When my mother was dying of cancer, and my little son was not quite so little any more, I felt totally poised between the generation that came before me and the generation that came after me in a way that I never had before – or since.

I sort of got it – the cycle of life thing. The way that, in the end, you lose everyone – your parents get old and die, your children grow up and leave you – and although it breaks your heart, it is the most natural thing in the world.

I knew I wanted to write something about all of this ordinary yet momentous stuff, something longer that maybe a few people would like – and even if nobody liked it except me, then I still had to write it. And that became the novel, *Man and Boy*.

I like writing about these things. About the way we break each other's hearts, sometimes without meaning to. It is endlessly fascinating. It is the most important part of our lives. It helps me make sense of the world, and my part of it.

My timing has always been a bit out. I was a young husband and father, and then I was a single dad for most of my thirties, and then I met Yuriko and got married at thirty-eight, became a dad again in my forties. It has been wonderful research, and I think that a writer can ask no more of his life.

As a reader, too, I always bought books that had something

to say about the great game – even if I couldn't always finish them.

I think that there are a lot of people like me. We want to understand the great game, we want to make sense of our lives – what could be more human than that? – and yet we know there is no magic handbook that explains everything. We muddle on. We make it up as we go along. With husbands and wives, lovers and partners, parents and children, the woman next door and the man at the gym.

So this book is for the people like me, the searching souls who bought *Men Are from Mars, Women Are from Venus* – but only read the first fifty pages.

And the title? This morning I sat on the steps of a Caribbean hotel room with my seven-year-old daughter, watching a mongoose chase a lizard around the trunk of a palm tree.

It went on for what seemed like ages but was probably only a minute or two – the mongoose inches from the tail of the lizard, the lizard running for its life. You could not look away. It was like being David Attenborough.

And my daughter, being seven and gentle of heart, is very sensitive to anything that smacks of unkindness to animals. She is always telling me that fast-food outlets should only use chickens and cows that have died of old age.

'That's so cruel,' she said, shaking her head as the mongoose and the lizard bombed around the palm tree.

'No,' I said. 'The mongoose has to hunt to survive. It's really not cruel – it's life and death.'

She looked at me, unconvinced, and I saw that it was a lousy answer. Because I had described the enormity of the moment – and the mongoose was getting ever closer to the lizard – but not how natural it was, how this kind of stuff happens every day, and has no choice – it has to happen every day.

The mongoose caught the lizard. It was over in a moment. We watched the mongoose sitting alone, at the bottom of the palm tree, smacking its lips.

'And he has to eat,' I said. 'The mongoose can't order from room service.'

My daughter nodded.

'Life, death and breakfast,' she said, and she seemed slightly happier with that.

Tony Parsons, 2010

One

The Mid-Life Myth

I was asked to go on one of those radio shows – you know, the kind where a bunch of middle-class, middle-aged pussies sit around whining about how hard it is for the modern male when his life approaches half-time.

The mid-life crisis – that hoary old chestnut. That complete fallacy. That shagged-out old cliché.

And I almost went. Because I felt like standing on the roof of Broadcasting House and screaming, What is wrong with you guys? Don't you know by now? Is it not as clear as the laughter lines on your face?

A man's life gets infinitely and immeasurably easier as he gets older.

Mid-life crisis? What mid-life crisis?

The mid-life crisis is a myth. More than this, the mid-life crisis is a lie. Life only gets better for men – better and better as the years roll by. Mid-life is not a crisis. Mid-life is when you are getting warmed up. When you have money in your pants. When you are doing a job you love. When you are an adorable combination of youth and experience. When you know how to find a clitoris without Google Earth.

So some thirty-nine-year-old man runs off with his secretary, or his neighbour's wife, or a Latvian lap dancer. So what? So some forty-four-year-old executive goes off on a business trip and ends up sampling more than the Toblerone in his mini-bar. So what? So a fifty-year-old guy decides he wants to trade in his Ford Fiasco for a Harley-Davidson. So what?

Every fifty-year-old man I know owns a Harley-Davidson. And they are all very happy. That's not a mid-life crisis. That's Me time. That's known as, for once in your life, doing exactly what you feel like doing.

What we call a mid-life crisis – it's tame stuff, isn't it? Changing your woman, changing your means of transport, changing your trousers . . .

This is not to suggest that these things can always be done without pain and tears. That Latvian lap dancer might leave you, or you might wrap your motorbike around a lamppost, or your Diesel Viker straight-leg jeans may be a sartorial disaster – mine were – but, compared to the poisoned chalice of youth, this is all just a pint of mild and bitter.

Unless a man has led an extraordinarily sheltered life, the so-called crisis of his middle years – whatever form it takes – will be nothing much compared to the crisis he faced down in young manhood.

I look back at my youth and I see . . . turmoil.

Drugs. Women. Fights. Drink. Ice cubes made from the tears of the broken-hearted. Often all in one lunch break.

And I remember friends dying. Not from the cancer and treacherous tickers that stalk us later in the unrelenting cycle of life but in all the raw violence of youth.

Dead in car crashes. Dead from drugs. My friend Johnny Thunders died in a New Orleans hotel at the age of thirty-eight – just when he should have been preparing for one of those mid-life clichés. If Johnny had lived, would he really have experienced a mid-life crisis? Would he have fretted about needing a size bigger in leather trousers, or why heroin didn't taste as good as it used to?

Whatever the middle years had in store for Johnny Thunders, it would have seemed pretty tame compared to the screaming insanity of what came before.

And hardly a crisis at all.

So it is for all of us. Youth is never a stroll in the park. It is almost always harder than what waits down the line. It is sad – tragic even – when a marriage breaks up, or when your hairline is receding faster than your career, or when love grows cold and beyond recall. But look on the bright side: is it really tougher than what you endured in your teens and twenties? Wanting a new car, or a new woman, or a new way of living – is it really such a crisis?

I would suggest not.

Where does it come from – this idea that a man reaches a certain point in his life when all is peaceful and calm? When there are no more irrational passions and unfulfilled yearn-ings, and no desire to – one last time – spill his seed on the passenger seat of some inappropriate ride?

'Stop dreaming of the quiet life, 'cos it's the one we'll never know,' sang the Jam when I was young, and I have always cherished the wisdom of those words.

A man never gets to a point when trouble of some shade or another is completely out of the picture. The mid-life crisis is born of the illusion that nothing exciting should happen to you once you are in the far-flung corners of youth.

And it is just not true.

What has gone wrong since I became a grown-up? Oh, the usual. Divorce. Bereavement. Money troubles. Promiscuity. Coveting my neighbour's wife. Coveting my neighbour's car. Coveting my neighbour's lawn mower. A bit more bereavement. A few more money troubles. Did I mention the coveting?

But none of these domestic nightmares – which began in my late twenties and went on for ten years or more – could be con-sidered a mid-life crisis. It was all just . . . *the stuff that happens in a lifetime.* And what doesn't kill you makes you stronger – unless it's a baseball bat or something.

In many ways, the middle bit of life is where we start getting it right. You get divorced – but then you meet someone love-lier, and you get married to her. Your parents die, but the years go by and you realise how lucky you were to have that woman as your mother and that man as your father.

You see that this is not a mid-life crisis at all. It is merely

Mother Nature doing what she is obliged to do: kick you firmly in the testicles.

As time goes by, inevitably you have a lot more money than you had when you were seventeen or twenty-one. Yet that does not stop the money troubles of your middle years from being as real as a tumour. So you grit your teeth, you do good work and – eventually – good things start to happen. The best things.

Life is infinitely better now than when I wore DMs every day of my life. At twenty-two I lived in a bedsit in Crouch End where you had to sleep on the right side of the mattress when it rained because water came through the ceiling. Even if it all falls apart tomorrow, even if I forget my name and have fragments of jam sponge cake on my unshaven chin, I am never going to live anywhere as rotten as that again.

Youth is hard for most of us. It is different for girls, but boys are often lonely because the girls their age want older boys – boys with money, boys with cars, boys who know how to talk to them.

Youth is frustrating. You are rarely doing the job you want and, in your late teens and early twenties, life can seem as though it is slipping away far more desperately than it ever does in your thirties and forties.

Mid-life crisis? You mean doing the job you love? You mean a ceiling that doesn't leak and a woman who loves you? You mean having a couple of quid in your pocket? You mean swapping the bus for a BMW X5 – and then swapping that for a Harley? Sounds pretty good to me, this mid-life crisis caper.

The trouble is that society confuses being a middle-aged man with being a freshly made corpse. A lot of what gets put down to a mid-life crisis is actually just a man revealing the first signs of life that he has shown in years.

I would never suggest that a man should give his heart to the first girl he meets who is young enough to be his daughter. And it is not a good idea to start riding motorbikes without having considered the possibility that you might fall off. But if you do, then don't beat yourself up. This is not a mid-life crisis – this is you, still breathing.

My father was a middle-aged man at twenty. He had killed many men and he had seen many men die. The top half of his body was a starburst of scar tissue. For the next forty years, until he died at the age of sixty-two, he had hard, black, jagged bits of shrapnel from a German grenade worming their way out of his legs. Still a young man, he wanted nothing more than to work, raise a family and tend his garden.

But even my dad – who often gave me the impression that he had had his fill of the outside world – discovered a new passion in his middle years.

He took up sailing. Every year he went down to Cowes, where he impressed the posh boys with his nautical skills. Was that a mid-life crisis? No, it was just my father rediscovering his passion for the open sea, and messing about in boats, and sailing. It was just my father remembering that he was alive, but he would not be forever. And of course it was a lot less trouble than having him elope with a Latvian lap dancer.

This is not to make the case that age is inherently better than youth. There are many slings and arrows in your middle years – the closer proximity of death, the way hangovers last for days, the desire of GPs to give you a prostate examination every time you bend over to tie your Asics trainers.

But where did it come from, this idea that there's a point in life when a man should stop seeking fulfilment, stop looking for meaning and stop having fun?

And when did we get it into our heads that at a certain stage in life troubles melt away, relationships stop falling apart and our hearts are no longer capable of ecstasy, or of breaking? That only happens on the day we die and until then life is full of varying measures of joy and pain, and it doesn't matter a damn whether you happen to be sporting a six-pack or a family pack.

The mid-life crisis is a myth designed to keep men tame, neutered and in their place. It doesn't exist. Fight against it. Buy a motorbike. Learn to play bass. Trek the Himalayas. Buy a Porsche 911. Learn Mandarin. Fall in love. Give up your job. Actually, better not give up your job – the passions that come later in life are only made possible because you are no longer on the tight budget of youth.

And there are plenty of middle-aged women who fancy a change of direction – or the bloke who lives down the street. There are plenty of women who get sick of their jobs, or their shagged-out old husbands, or who want to dance the Tango in Buenos Aires before they die. And why not? Let there be fire in your eyes and flashing limbs. Dump the husband. Fly to Argentina. Enjoy every sandwich. You're a long time cremated.

But somehow it is only a mid-life crisis when a man does it – when he decides that, now he comes to think of it, he doesn't want to be a chartered accountant. He wants to kiss the face of God.

We should all be allowed to kiss the face of God, whether it comes in the form of a bigger bike or a younger lover or the rolling sea. How else to respond to our mortality?

There is no cure for death, no age limit for dreams, and no escape from who we are and always will be – mortal, fallible creatures, full of love and longing.

And if the young lover breaks your heart, or if you fall off your Harley, or if Buenos Aires is a disappointment – if you make a fool of yourself – well, that is what we do, and what we have always done.

That is not a mid-life crisis.

It's just the latest in a long line of cock-ups.

Two

When Yobs Swear

Sooner or later you will find yourself in a situation. It may not happen for ten years. It could be tonight. But it is coming – be sure of that – and when it arrives you will have the choice between the only two buttons that really matter on your biological dashboard.

Fight or flight?

You might be in a bar. You might be in a restaurant. It could be at the end of your road or it could be on a tropical island. You might be standing outside your home. The location doesn't matter. This is how it will be: you will be confronted by inappropriate behaviour that intrudes upon those you love. Effing and blinding and talk of a graphically sexual nature. You know the kind of thing. And, in an instant, you will have to decide – Do I say something?

Or do I say nothing?

This is the terrible thing. This is the heart of the matter. You will not be alone. You will be in company – with your girlfriend or wife, or with your children, even if they have yet to be born – people who look to you to protect them from the worst of this world.

And there will be a cackling mob of pimply cavemen, every other gormless word an expletive, talking about bitches and blow-jobs and easy birds. They will bring their world into your world and you will have to decide, in a terrifying instant, what to do.

Even if what you do is nothing.

You can get killed for saying something. Even a mild rebuke can get you the death sentence, effective immediately. Men die for speaking up.

But these lads are *loud* – too loud to be ignored. By you or your woman or your child. Do you want your kid to listen to this stuff? Or do you risk making him or her an orphan?

Yobs are so touchy these days, that's the problem. Yobs are more sensitive than they have ever been in yob history. They react to the mildest rebuke with murderous rage. The average hoodie is thin-skinned beyond belief, his self-esteem so fragile that any criticism is almost guaranteed to explode into physical confrontation.

One thing is certain: reasoning with them does not work. Appealing to their better nature is a waste of time – they don't have one. If, when yobs swear, you tell them to turn down the volume, you'd better be prepared to go all the way.

Because they will be.

Context is everything. I don't advocate going around telling every foul-mouthed moron to shut his filthy cakehole. It does not bother me at all if I am at a football match and the bloke in the seat behind me is shouting about 'stupid cunts'. The stupid cunts at football matches don't bother me. I don't much care what anyone says if I am alone. But if I am out with my family and it happens – in a restaurant, in a park, in a hotel bar – then that's different.

Nothing will get me to keep my mouth shut. And it is nothing to do with bravery. I just can't accept foul-mouthed strangers entering my daughter's world. And I am very happy to kick, gouge and claw while rolling in the dirt to make my point.

Stupid, really. I am not much good to my daughter if some psycho-chav buries his blade in my heart. And what a waste – to lose your life because you asked some pathetic piece of pond scum – and his mates, because they are invariably mob-handed – to watch his potty mouth.

But there is nothing rational about the flight-or-fight mechanism. It is not a debating society. It is not as though you carefully weigh the options and then go with one or the other. The moment you make your decision is here and gone before you know it.

And suddenly you are either bowing your craven head because safety is the wisest course of action, or you are confronting a group of leering teenagers – because sometimes the stupid thing is also the right thing.

And then you ask yourself: Can I take them? These leering strangers – will they put me in the A&E or the graveyard?

Almost certainly, all things considered, you can't take them. They are younger than you, stronger than you, and you are the one who is flying solo. They are what the media call multiple assailants.

But what gets you through is that – if you are mad enough to say something in the first place – you are inevitably a lot angrier than they are.

You come out of nowhere, seething with rage, right in their faces – they haven't been *trying* to offend your small child. You're ready to rumble, full of that righteous, blood-pumping juice where you just don't care what happens to you. And that might just be enough to make them back down and go away, despite their superior numbers.

If they don't kill you, that is.

They killed young Kevin Johnson. He was twenty-two years old, at home in Sunderland with his seven-month-old baby son Chase trying to sleep in his cot. It was the early hours of the morning. And down on the street, right outside Kevin's front door, a gang of lads was getting very loud. Kevin could have put the pillow over his head. He could have tried to soothe his son. He could have done nothing. That would have been the easiest thing to do. But Kevin went out into the street and told the gang – there were three of them – to keep the noise down. And they stabbed him to death. And Chase Johnson will grow up without a father because Kevin refused to take the soft, sensible option. Because Kevin Johnson was decent. Because Kevin Johnson was brave. Because Kevin Johnson wanted to protect his family. No doubt Chase will be proud of his father one day. And so he should be. Even if he will never remember him.

Entitlement – that's the great curse of our age. Every scabby little yob thinks he has the right to do whatever he wants at whatever volume he wants. Nobody has any responsibility to the wider community. And that's what it comes down to when you tell some foul-mouthed gang to cut it out. You are saying: I'm here too, I have rights too. A crazy thing to say in this day and age.

In *Brokeback Mountain*, Heath Ledger's character Ennis is at a Fourth of July party with his wife and two small daughters when a couple of bikers start making a loud comparative study of 'pussy' in Montana and Wyoming.

'Let's move, Ennis, let's just move,' says his wife, Alma. But Ennis is a man not a mouse and he quietly and politely asks the two drunken bikers to 'Keep it down – I got two little girls here.'

They don't just ignore him. They start loudly speculating about the last time Ennis had sex with his missus. They provoke him. They goad him. They are unrepentant in their obscenities. They can't get past the pussy. It's pussy, pussy, pussy with these guys. And they tell him to listen to his wife: if he doesn't like it, then go sit somewhere else.

Ennis goes wild. He kicks the first biker full in the face, knocking him out cold, and offers to put the other one's teeth in his digestive system. The conscious biker backs away, dragging his bloodied pal with him.

And what makes the scene a work of genius is that Ennis' wife and children are not grateful. Far from it.

They are all appalled at the violence that lurks inside this soft-spoken husband and devoted father. As several families pick up their blankets and move away – as if it is Ennis who poses a threat to civilisation, rather than the bikers – his children whimper and hide and his wife stares at him as if seeing him for the first time.

In my experience, that's just what it is like.

When yobs swear, it is very easy to end up looking like the bad guy. It is very easy to find your wife and child staring at you as if they have suddenly realised that you are, in fact, a gay cowboy.

This is how it was. We were in a restaurant. At the next table were three teenage lads. They were probably not so different to me and my mates at that age – although I don't recall sitting around in family restaurants in my teens. And they were discussing the sister of one of the lads. 'A right little slag', apparently. 'She was ready to give him a jump!' This was said while gesturing at one of the group – presumably not her brother, though you never know.

I listened to this stuff for, oh, about four minutes, or possibly six, as my wife pretended to study the menu and our small daughter crayoned in her *My Little Pony* workbook.

Then I told them to shut the fuck up.

And I told them that I was only going to give them one fucking warning. And – red-faced with rage, ludicrously holding a knife and fork in my hand, as though I might eat them alive – I pointed at my daughter and said that she wasn't going to listen to this fucking stuff about how your fucking sister was ready to fuck anybody, for fuck's sake.

They were scared. They shut up and ate their happy meals

as quiet as mice. And I know they could have beaten the living shit out of me with absolutely no problem. I would have had no chance whatsoever against multiple assailants of their age and size. But here's the thing: it mattered more to me than it did to them. And I really meant it. If they had told me to go fuck myself, I would have happily kicked them through the buffet bar. Or attempted to.

As soon as I told them to shut up, they were not the problem. The problem was my wife. She pointed out – later, when we were alone, when that miserable meal was over – that our daughter had been so busy colouring in the *My Little Pony* characters that she had not heard a word they had said about the slutty sister. But – so my wife insisted – our daughter had heard every profanity spat out by her psychotic father.

When yobs swear, you sort of hope that your family will love you more if you make a stand. You hope they will be grateful that you are the kind of man who does not just turn his butt cheeks and say, Go ahead, world, fuck me up the arse.

You think they might even be proud of you.

Not a bit of it. Like Alma, the wife in *Brokeback Mountain*, my own wife was horrified by the level of rage I had to summon up before I could say anything. My wife was as appalled as Heath Ledger's missus in *Brokeback Mountain*. And I am not even having a secret affair with Jake Gyllenhaal.

But the truth is, we do not do it for them. The brutal fact of the matter is that – if we are one of the fools who dares to speak up – we are doing it almost exclusively for ourselves.

Our women – those pragmatic girlfriends, those hard-headed wives – think that ultimately it is not worth it. Risking your life for a random bout of inappropriate behaviour? That's the madness of the macho man. I personally think that men like Kevin Johnson are modern-day heroes and we could use a million more just like him. But his son will miss his father every day of his life, and at some point he will have the right to ask, *But was it worth it, Dad?*

Fight or flight? These two disparate instincts have the same function: to save your hide. But sometimes doing nothing, while saving your life, robs you of your soul.

Ultimately, the only argument that matters is about the kind of man you want to be. And when did we stop being the kind of men who want to protect the people we love? When did that go out of style? When did wanting to protect your family become old-fashioned?

My old martial arts teacher had a wonderful recipe for dealing with trouble. 'Walk away,' he would tell me, after hundreds of hours spent teaching me to kick and punch and block. 'Walk away.'

Yeah but no but, I would say to him. But he had heard it all before, and he believed that none of it was worth killing or dying for. Someone spills your drink? Walk away. Someone bumps into you? Walk away. And it's true – most trouble you can just walk away from. You can smile. You can apologise. You can put the pillow over your head.

But there comes a point when walking away means that

you will think yourself less of a man. For most of us, that moment comes when some careless stranger is far too close to our women and our children. And I don't walk away from that – whatever the wife wants. That's where I stand and I draw the line and I get ready to roll around on the floor of the restaurant.

I don't want any trouble. Honestly. Really. But it's just like Ennis says in *Brokeback Mountain*:

'You need to shut your slop-bucket mouths – you hear me?'

Three

Dying Parents

If you only see two dead bodies in your life, then make sure they are your parents.

The death of a mother or father cannot be grasped from a distance. The phone call, the sealed coffin – it's not enough to comprehend that kind of loss – that twice-in-a-lifetime loss.

Inevitable it may be, but the death of a parent has an unimaginable quality to it. You need to see for yourself that they are truly gone, to understand that the ones who brought you into this world have gone from this world. So go look at the body. That is not the end of losing your father or mother. But that is where it begins.

Even as the numbing bureaucracy of death clamours for your attention – the funeral arrangements, deciding what to do with the leftovers of a lifetime, the surreal task of choosing a coffin – would Dad like the simple pine number, or the Napoleon job with the brass handles? – you have to force yourself to go and see.

To the hospital. To the undertaker's back room. Or – if they died at home, as my mother did – then to the master bedroom of the house where you grew up.

It helps. More than this, it is necessary. Yet viewing the dead body of a parent is a curiously flat experience. You feel it should be charged with emotion. There should be hot tears, and some final embrace, and Katherine Jenkins singing, 'Time to Say Goodbye'.

But the emotion comes earlier – in the cancer ward, in the hospital café, sitting by the death bed drinking endless cups of bad tea – and it comes later – at the funeral, or when you go through dusty cupboards, and your dead dad's clothes, or your mother's heartbreaking jewellery, or their photograph albums, and it takes you many strange hours to realise the obvious.

Everything must go.

Those are the moments for the spikes of emotion. But when you summon up the nerve to gaze upon your dead parent – as you have to, as you must – you hardly recognise them. You even feel a bit cheated. Mum? Dad? Where are you?

And it is not because the undertaker has weaved his crafty embalming magic, or that a mouth is set in a line that you never saw in life. It is simply because the spark has flown. The thing that made that woman your mother, or made that man your father, has gone forever. And you don't know if they have gone to a better place, or into black oblivion.

But that is not he. And that is not she.

You must look at the face of your dead parent not because it gives you a chance to say some last farewell but because until you do you will never even begin to understand that they are dead, and that you are alone in this world as you have never been alone before.

And even then it is hard. Even then it is next to impossible. Last month my mother had been gone for ten years. Ten years since the cancer overwhelmed her. Ten years since I returned to my home from her home to search for a hospice, leaving her in the care of an elderly friend, an ex-nurse – lovely Nelly, now gone herself – and got the call in the middle of the night to say come as fast you can. And it still wasn't fast enough. Ten years dead – and yet, here's the funny thing: I recently tried to call her.

I actually reached for the phone to relate some news that I knew would make her smile, and then I stopped myself, thinking – mental or what?

I got there not long after she died, and kissed her face, and saw an expression on that face that I had never seen when she lived, and yet it is still hard to believe.

Yet here is what you learn. There are two ways for your parents to die – quickly and slowly.

They go quick. They go slow.

But they go.

My dad was quick. My mum was slow.

My dad had lung cancer for a year and – being the hardest bastard in the universe – told nobody about it. His lungs were being eaten away and we never knew. Then one day he collapsed, was rushed to hospital and three weeks later we buried him.

A decade and a bit later, my mum had the same kind of cancer for the same length of time, but I was by her side and holding her hand when some busy NHS doctor told her there was no more they could do. And then she talked about it, and she weighed her chances of survival, and she confronted terminal illness with the combination of humour and grit that was peculiar to her generation of war brides. It was a very different experience to watching my dad go. But then she died too.

And I thought that the world should stop. Let me catch my breath. Acknowledge the passing of this woman – five feet nothing of bravery and jokes, even when the doctors were solemnly shaking their heads, and slyly looking at their fucking watches. It is only now I see the obvious.

Losing your parents is the most natural thing in the world.

And of course there are far worse things in this life than watching a parent die. Some people have to bury a child. Many people bury a spouse. Losing a parent is surely just another season, one more turn in the cycle of life.

Yet the world seems to change. First one goes, then the other.

'You're an orphan now,' more than one person told me when my parents were both gone, and I thought that was a tad dramatic. I don't see how a grown man can be an orphan.

It is completely natural to lose your parents. We all have our time. And then it's up.

Then why does something so natural feel so completely and brutally unnatural?

You never know when they are going to go. Forget all that three-score-years-and-ten bullshit. I have a friend who lost his father before he was born. I have other friends who lost parents in childhood. I even have a friend who, when she was a girl, lost both of her parents in the same car crash – an incredibly common experience, as it turns out, because husbands and wives – fathers and mothers – regularly share a car.

Yet I have other friends well into middle age who still have both their parents living. And I have noted that the longer your parents live, the tougher it becomes to let go of them. You would think it would be the other way round – that spending almost half a century with your parents would make you more prepared to let go. But it doesn't work that way.

And whenever they die – if your father goes when you are still in your mother's womb, or if your mother goes when you see a middle-aged man you don't recognise staring back at you from the shaving mirror – the world changes. There is nothing like the death of a parent to help you see the big picture, to truly get it, for the very first time. How could you have missed something so obvious?

Golden lads and girls all must
As chimney sweepers, come to dust.

When you bury your parents, you pull down the barrier between yourself and mortality.

When the first parent goes, the Earth shifts. When the second one goes, the Earth falls apart. When my father died in 1987, my mother left his suits untouched. She slept on her side of the bed. She stayed in the same house – for twelve years and one day – until her own death.

But when the surviving parent goes, the last link to your youth goes with her. Those strange hours spent wandering an empty house, opening drawers, peering into a vanished life, working out what to keep – what is priceless – and what to leave out for the bin men. It is the photo albums that do you in. Not because of all those familiar faces but because of all the faces that you do not know, as the memories of a lifetime dissolve like teardrops in the rain.

You don't really know your parents until you watch them die. My father was the toughest man I ever knew, and then I saw him in that cancer ward, shot full of morphine, and he was afraid. I was shocked. I had never seen him afraid before, that scarred old soldier. I didn't think he was capable of fear. That's how little I knew him.

And my mum was a typical post-war housewife, as placidly faithful as a woman in a Tammy Wynette song.

Everyone thought she would just wither away with her husband gone, this man she had been with since she was sixteen and he was seventeen. And she didn't.

She discovered some inner steel. She realised she had an army of friends. She even learned that loneliness had its compensations. She could play her country and western records very loudly, without my dad shaking his *Daily Express* with irritation.

When your parents are around – giving or denying approval to boy and man, diminishing you with just one look or a few sharp words when you break a window, or drop out of school, or get divorced – there are powerful forces preventing you from reaching true maturity. You are still some kind of child until both of your parents are dead. You don't know them until they are dying and you don't know yourself.

For most of us, losing a parent is our first real contact with death. Until then, death is an impossibly distant prospect, and we kid ourselves that it can be kept at bay forever if we eat up our greens.

We live in a death-free culture. If you make it out of the womb you are likely to survive childhood. There are no world wars. Your fussy modern car scolds you if you fail to wear your seat belt.

You think you have time to burn until your parents are dying. Then for the first time in your life, your own death is undeniable.

When your parents are alive, you believe you will live forever. From the moment they die, you start counting the years that you have left.

The classic text on bereavement, *On Death and Dying*, by Elisabeth Kübler-Ross, cites the five stages all men must stop at on their path to death.

First stage – denial and isolation.
Second stage – anger.
Third stage – bargaining.
Fourth stage – depression.
Fifth stage – acceptance.

What is true of the dying is true of the ones left behind. You get over it. You do. With time, scar tissue covers the deepest wounds. You become grateful that this man was your father, that this woman was your mother. You learn to feel blessed for what you had, rather than rail at what has been lost.

Yet you never really get used to it. In an unguarded moment – always some happy moment, when I have some small good news to relate – I am capable of reaching for the phone to call a woman who died in the last century.

Maybe she is watching down. Or maybe not. When I kissed the cheek of my dead mother – already cold, already departed, already truly not her – I did not know if she had gone to heaven, or simply gone. There were no clues.

Only when your parents die do you realise that the clock is running like the meter of a bent mini-cab driver – and it's running for you. And whatever comes after this short sweet life, be it heavenly hosts or a dreamless void or some great eternal kip, it will not be long until you find out for yourself.

Four

Angry Old Man

You never argue at airport security. And then one day
you do.

You never argue at airport security because those lethargic,
blank-eyed men and women are the front line in the war on
terror. You never argue at airport security because it is pointless, and they are just doing a job, and the stupid questions –
Is this your toothpaste, sir? – and the dumb rituals – they find
one shoe bomber and so all of mankind has to take off its
footwear until the end of days – are the price we pay for
pretending we are safe.

And then one day you snap.

For me it was Frankfurt, when they confiscated the entire
contents of my toilet bag – yes, I bet that had old Osama trembling in his cave – and then gave me some insolent lip when
I mildly commented that I had lugged all that stuff through
Heathrow without anyone raising an eyebrow.

'Ja,' said the sausage-munching jobsworth. 'But here ve haf
rules.'

I gawped. I laughed. And then I pointed out that back in

the sleepy little place that I come from – London town, Fritz, perhaps you've heard of it – ve also haf rules.

'And the reason we have rules,' I continued, 'is because for about seventy years we have had somebody trying to blow us to pieces. Right now it is Islamic nutjobs, but before that we had thirty years of the IRA and before that – I hate to bring it up – it was the Luftwaffe.' I cackled with derisive laughter. 'But if confiscating my Gillette Sensitive Skin Shaving Foam makes the fatherland a safer place, then *bitte schoen,* be my guest.'

Oh, it was an ugly scene. I was too loud. I was too mouthy. But all the pointless bossiness that I have experienced at airports all over the world finally reached critical mass. And I blew. And as I walked away with what remained of my personal belongings – dirty socks and a pair of rusty tweezers – I realised that I had become something I never thought I would be.

I had turned into an angry old man.

We think of rage as being the province of the young. We think of youth as being the age of righteous, red-blooded protest. But the young are not angry any more. The young of the twenty-first century are a placid, bovine, docile bunch, sucking up the Arctic Monkeys on their iPods, dreaming of catching Simon Cowell's eye.

They might fret about the environment, but they are not angry about it – not really. They might be a bit miffed about what we get up to in our distant wars, but I don't see them marching to Downing Street or rioting in Grosvenor Square. They might get a bit trembly-chinned over Third World poverty, but they think that watching Coldplay in Hyde Park and flashing their student union Visa card will wipe away Africa's tears.

The young are no longer capable of anger. If you want to see genuine fury at the way of the world, then look at a man on the far side of thirty. And as he gets older – thirty-one, thirty-two, forty, fifty – the anger builds. By the time I am sixty I confidently expect to be on the roof of a public building somewhere with a high-powered rifle while the neighbours reflect, 'Well, he was always a bit of a loner.'

Nothing makes a young man angry.

Everything makes an old man angry.

I can no longer go to the cinema. I just get too angry – angry at the sound of some barnyard pal chewing cud in the seat behind me, angry at the dozy bastards staring into the wintry glow of their mobile phones, as though they would vanish in a puff of smoke if they turned off the Nokia for two hours. And talking during the movie – well, that puts me in a state that is somewhere beyond mere anger. If you ever saw someone in a cinema suddenly shove his face into someone else's face and scream at the very top of his voice, 'SHUT THE FUCK UP!' then that might have been me. I know you are meant to clear your throat in a disapproving fashion, or mutter a sharp, 'Sssh!' But I can't seem to do any of that. I wish I could. But there's too much blood pumping through my veins for a quick, 'Ssssh!'

I scream. I rave. And if the barnyard pal is sitting directly in front of me, then I kick his seat with the heel of my boot as hard as I possibly can, and when he turns around I scream, 'SHUT THE FUCK UP!'

Then of course you have to be prepared to roll around in the aisle of a cinema, sticky with popcorn and spilled soda pop. There are twenty movies that I have paid to see that I have no idea how they ended. Because I was waiting to be joined in mortal combat.

But what can I do? I am an angry old man.

So no cinema for me – and countless nights out ruined for my loved ones, because something – cud chewing, mobile gazing, mindless chatter in the darkness – set me off.

But I am not a single-issue angry person. Almost everything makes me angry these days. I am angry at people who litter. Yet I am also angry at people who want to force me to recycle. I am angry at people who have no manners, and I am angry at people who swear around children, and I am angry at people in Smart cars, who inevitably drive in an incredibly stupid fashion. People, really – I am angry at people. Any kind of rudeness, finger wagging or ignorance is liable to light my blue touch paper.

Sometimes I think of Terry in *The Likely Lads*, who did not like foreigners, or southerners or – now he thought about it – the bloke next door. But the anger that comes to us all with time is not mere misanthropy – this is not anger for anger's sake.

It is hard-earned, clear-eyed and horribly justified.

You have seen too much. You have lived too long. You know the way things should work, and you are maddened by the yawning chasm between your expectations and the grim reality of the workaday world.

I don't want to be this way. I want to be happy. I want to be nice. I want to be like the kid I was as a young journalist, who was so happy to be flying to America to go on the road with Thin Lizzy that he truly didn't care that the plane sat on the runway at Heathrow for six hours, and didn't care that he was in economy. I didn't even know that I was in economy. I wasn't aware that planes had a class system. To me there were only seats on planes, and they were all good ones.

As my legs throbbed merrily with Deep Vein Thrombosis, I didn't care about anything at all apart from the fact that within twenty-four hours I would be immersed in the fleshpots of Philadelphia. Will I ever be that carefree and giddy with happiness again? Probably not. There is too much anger in me now. If an airline had me sitting on the runway for six hours today, my head would explode. They wouldn't be able to placate me with some savoury nuts.

My family stayed at the hotel that featured so glamorously in the James Bond film, *Casino Royale*: the One and Only Ocean Club in the Bahamas. And I say – be thankful there's only one of them. What a dump. It took us hours to check in and, you'll never guess, but that really made me angry.

Because I know that if you stay at the Sandy Lane in Barbados, or the Ritz-Carlton in Hong Kong, or the Jalousie Plantation in St Lucia, or the Conrad in Tokyo – or any other world-class five-star hotel that is worthy of the name and those five stars – they will check you in up in your room. Not the One and Only in the Bahamas. With our jet-lagged nipper in tow, we waited for literally hours to check in.

'You're always angry,' my wife told me. 'Why are you always so angry?'

'Because I know how things should work,' I replied, through gritted teeth.

And that's the problem. When you are young, you have no idea how the world should work. For most of my twenties, I thought that a mini-bar was the height of sophistication and luxury. Of course I was never angry – I was too grateful to be on the loose in the world, and I was too stupid. Anger comes with experience, anger comes with wisdom. What's true is that – righteous and justified though it may be – anger spoils everything.

'Why can't we just sit here and enjoy the sunset?' asked my saintly wife, as she cradled our exhausted daughter, and the staff of the One and Only Hellhole Bahamas gave us some more feeble excuses about why our room wasn't ready. 'It's such a beautiful sunset,' Yuriko said. 'Why can't we just enjoy it?'

Why not indeed? Why not contemplate the lovely sunset and count our blessings? Why bother to burst a blood vessel because of the failings of the international tourist trade?

It is a male thing. This dissatisfaction, this anger, this railing at the sloppy and the stupid and the sub-standard – it comes with your biological hard drive. It is wired into us, this rage to make right the world – or at least get dummies to stop looking at their mobile phones in the cinema.

It is the impulse that helped our species to crawl out of the primordial swamp. It is the reason the human race survived. It is the life-affirming core of everything.

No point in giving yourself a heart attack because some airport security dimwit who couldn't make it as a traffic warden confiscates your eye drops. No point in having an aneurysm because some gum-chewing simpleton is texting on his mobile during the third act of *The Departed*. No point in having a brain haemorrhage because you arrive at your hotel and your room doesn't have a chocolate on the pillow.

But only young men fresh from having their laundry done by Mum have any excuse to tolerate the world in all its venality and stupidity. The grown men know better – they have been around, and seen it all before, and we know that if you save up and splash out for two weeks in the One and Only Ocean Club, Bahamas, and your room is not ready when you arrive, then you have every right to blow a gasket. In fact, you are showing exemplary restraint worthy of Mahatma Gandhi and Martin Luther King by not smashing up their lobby. I will never again be that twenty-two-year-old, stunned by the sight of an economy seat and a mini bar, excited by the thought of seeing Thin Lizzy in Philadelphia, and I can't pretend otherwise.

The trouble is, there's no end to the anger. You get in your car – and you want to kill someone. You go through airport security – and someone who has never actually made anyone more secure starts bossing you around. You go to the cinema – and then one day you can't go to the cinema any more.

When does it end? It doesn't. The rage comes as youth goes and we shall never be free of it. It feels like an ancient emotion, a hereditary anger – something that has been handed down through generations of men, a bug-eyed fury passed down from angry grandfather to angry father to angry son.

I can't help feeling that the anger is somewhat wasted on the generations born in the second half of the twentieth century. I can't help believing that this rage was used for more constructive purposes in the past – to fight for survival, to free the world, to build better lives for people with nothing.

Perhaps male rage will die out with time. Perhaps decades of peace and prosperity will make the anger fall away, like a coat of fur on Neanderthal man, or a set of fins that are no longer needed on dry land. Perhaps angry men will disappear into history – like men in hats, and men in uniform. But not yet. And not for you and not for me. For us there can be only one honest response to cruelty and wickedness and stupidity, and people who don't say please or thank you.

Grumble, old man, grumble.

Five

Fear of Fake Breasts

Until a man has actually made love to a woman with fake breasts, he can never really know what they are like.

Round, juicy and tempting they may be.

But then so is a bowl of plastic fruit.

For no matter how good they look, the spell is broken the moment they are touched by human hands. The real things somehow manage to be both firm and soft, they feel undeniably human, they move, they are alive.

In comparison, counterfeit breasts feel as though they have been stolen from the morgue. Replicant breasts are so hard. Bogus breasts are so numb, so lifeless, so dead. Once they are outside the two dimensions of celebrity magazines, a pair of phonies are suddenly a million light years away from the objects they seek to imitate.

And real breasts are warm. The fake breasts I have encountered have always seemed cold to me, but that may have been my appalled imagination. Certainly you will get the best out of them if you look but don't touch.

But then that's almost the point of fake breasts. They are

not there to be fondled, kissed or felt, they are there to be admired, discussed, lusted after and photographed.

The moment they are touched – and I mean in the heat of passion, rather than out of curiosity or in the interests of scientific research – then the spell is broken. And this is true of all fake breasts, no matter how much money has been spent on this act of female self-mutilation.

Some women have reconstruction forced upon them. I watched my wife's mother die of breast cancer. The battles that women like my wife's mother have fought are insulted by the pumped-up twiglets on the cover of *Heat*.

The women who survive breast cancer – and even today, only lung and colon cancer kill more – are faced with hard choices. A lumpectomy – breast-conserving surgery – has to be followed with radiation treatment. A mastectomy – total removal of a breast – can be followed by reconstruction. But that means yet more surgery. These are all devastating choices for any woman.

But the overwhelming majority of women who have breast enhancement do not do it because they have fought cancer. They do it because of vanity. They do it because it has become a fashion option. They do it because they have an IQ somewhat smaller than their bra size.

And the brutal irony is that breast enhancement – boob jobs, in the baby talk that portrays it as akin to a getting a spray-on tan – makes everything from a benign lump to a malignant tumour infinitely harder to detect.

You would think that would be enough to put anyone off. And yet somehow it isn't.

In a bar at the end of the world, there was a story they told of a man who loved a dancer although the dancer could not love herself.

She was a great dancer, and most nights of the week, if you were in that club at the rough end of a rough street in that rough city, you might see her. And if you saw her dance once, then you would never forget her.

Physically, there was not much of her. She had the natural-born dancer's lack of waste. This man loved to look at her, and he thought that she was an undeniably beautiful woman. But – like many women who are told they are beautiful by men who have only just met them – she disagreed. The dancer had what a head doctor would call 'body issues'.

She was small-breasted. That was the heart of her complaint about herself. The man had always liked her exactly as she was, and thought she was perfect – but these small breasts were a big thing for her, an insurmountable barrier between her and true happiness.

She had great legs, a great little bum, a lovely face – but in her mind it all added up to nothing because of her small breasts. She started talking about her breasts more and more – how she would have more confidence if they were bigger, how she would dance better, how she would finally reach a point in her life when she felt good about herself.

She wanted surgery.

Naturally, he told her that he thought she looked great already. And he meant it. But it became clear that what he thought really didn't come into it.

She wouldn't be doing it for him.

She would be doing it for herself.

And he thought that made sense – it was her body and she was free to do what she liked with it. And also he was young and dumb – he didn't realise how the surgery would change everything between them.

So he got the money and gave it to her. He did it because he loved her. Then he went away. And when he came back to her town, he watched her dance and he drank his San Miguel and then he held her hand all the way home.

And – how stupid was this man? – he only realised that he was having sex with a woman with fake breasts after the moment of penetration. He had not noticed them when she was dancing.

But now he noticed them, because he could hardly miss them. They did not feel even remotely real. They felt as inauthentic as alcohol-free lager or sugar-free sweetener. Even faker than that – because they were no substitute for the real thing. They were impostors.

How unnatural those breasts felt in his hands and mouth, how bogus on the tip of his tongue, how *hard* pressed against his chest – that's the thing that shocked him most of all, the knock-on-wood hardness of the bloody things.

She had ruined herself. Really, he could not think of it any other way. Her silhouette now had something of the pouter pigeon about it. It broke his heart to see what she had done.

He did not stop loving her.

But they never made love again.

Why aren't there armies of thinking women protesting about the grotesquely booming trade in bogus breasts? Why don't women's magazines stop slavishly printing pictures of pumped-up stars with their pathetic plastic tits sticking out? Is it because to really and truly know how rotten fake breasts are, you have to be a heterosexual man?

Buying off-the-peg breasts is becoming as acceptable as a woman colouring her hair or whitening her teeth. But it is of a totally different order. There is something obscene about seeing healthy young women mutilate themselves by stuffing two plastic bags full of gel into their breasts. Having a 'boob job' – society's coy euphemism that hides the scarring, the risks to long-term health, and most of all the way good breasts get so casually traded for bad – is far closer to female circumcision than it is to any kind of cosmetic surgery.

But they look nice – right, girls?

'There are so many images of women with amazing fake boobs, I didn't think mine were good enough,' said Jodie Marsh, at the grand unveiling of her new, allegedly improved 32GG superboobs. 'I think society has forgotten what real boobs look like, and women like me end up thinking our boobs aren't nice because they disappear into our armpits when we lie down.'

And now Jodie's 'boobs' can point at the chandelier until the end of days. And I ask you – is that really better than breasts that can move around of their own free will?

Some of the most written about women in the country – Victoria Beckham, Jordan and Kerry Katona – have given Mother Nature a helping hand in the breast department. No doubt this love of fake breasts among the rich and famous (not to mention ageing and constantly photographed) is directly linked to a record number of teenagers having breast-enlargement surgery.

They don't know what they are letting themselves in for.

There are plenty of female celebrities with healthy breasts that do not feel like a sailor's wooden leg – off the top of my head, I think of Kate Moss, Sienna Miller and Leona Lewis – but unfortunately no operation exists to artificially inflate an insecure young woman's self-esteem.

'My boob job made me feel better,' says *EastEnders* actress Lacey Turner.

What she means is that the operation made her feel better *about herself*. Trust me on this one, Lacey – no boob job ever made a woman feel better.

Don't do it, girls. Renounce all breast enlargement. Turn your back, and your breasts, on that surgeon's knife. If not for your man, then for your health. These breast-job babes blow my mind – these are women who would not dream of smoking a cigarette or going to the beach without sun block, yet they willingly undergo surgery that practically guarantees a health hazard in coming years.

Those vain – or insecure, or neurotic, or self-loathing – women willingly risk infection, breast pain, changes in nipple sensitivity, visible wrinkling, complications with breast feeding and asymmetric appearance (i.e. breasts so completely different that they resemble the brothers played by Arnold Schwarzenegger and Danny de Vito in *Twins*).

And what they never tell you in the celebrity rags is that off-the-shelf breasts can rupture.

You can give it a fancy name like mammoplasty enlargement or augmentation mammoplasty, but in the end it is just a bog standard boob job where a silicone shell is filled with either gel or sterile saline liquid and stuffed inside a woman's breasts via various types of incision.

Inframammary incisions are inserted under the breast, and make a woman look like she has had some terrible domestic accident. Periareolar incisions go in through the nipple, which leaves less scarring but increases the risk of capsular contracture, when the body's immune system tries to repel what it sees as a foreign invader.

There are other incisions – the transaxillary goes in through the armpit, the transabdominoplasaty through the stomach and the transumbilical goes in through the navel.

They all hurt like hell.

I have never met a woman who did not find breast enlargement the most painful experience of their life – including childbirth and watching their boyfriends dance at weddings. But this initial pain is likely to be just the start of her problems.

Those silicone shells can break, leak or slip. A woman can be left with her nipples pointing in different directions. Breast sensitivity often goes out the window when a woman goes for the fake boob option. The pain she feels after the operation can endure for years – perhaps forever.

It spoils sex for the man. And for the woman too.

So that's sex spoilt for everyone then.

But last year in America alone, nearly half a million women had breast-enlargement surgery. I would suggest that not one of them is the woman they were before – imperfect perhaps, but with a natural beauty that no plastic surgeon could ever improve upon.

And speaking purely from the male perspective, sex with a woman wearing replicant breasts is no fun. That's the vicious punchline – there's this mirage of perfection, this pert promise of ultimate pleasure, and the vision evaporates the moment you reach out to touch them.

Fake breasts are the cock-tease from hell.

The dancer's breasts were well done. On an objective level, the man could see that the surgery had been efficiently performed. There was none of the horrific scarring on the underside of the breasts that he had seen elsewhere. And yet they repelled him.

As well done as they were, these fake breasts did not belong on a real woman. They were artificially created monsters from some doctor's menu of butchery.

In the cold light of day, she looked like a porn fantasy – sporting replicants that were there to attract, to be looked at, leered over, lusted after and remembered. But they were not really there to be touched.

They were not there for any man who might love this woman, or for any baby she might give birth to. It felt like those breasts were there for the rest of the world.

Don't do it, girls.

Love what God gave you, no matter how much or how Double-AA. Small can be fun. Medium can be lovely. Large can be grand. Those hard, fake things are always awful. Do you really want to present those lifeless objects to the man you love? Do you really want to shove some surgeon's rock-hard creation in your baby's face?

Fake breasts desecrate a woman's body. Fake breasts take the joy of sex and pump it full of lifeless gel. Fake breasts look bad, feel bad and will one day make you sick. And they are so horribly, unforgivably dangerous.

Keep your health, keep your self-respect, keep your man. It should not take a man to tell you – learn to love yourself the way you are.

Keep them real.

Six

Humiliation

In my first year at school, my little chums played a wonderful joke on me. 'I know,' they giggled. 'When we get changed for PE, let's get Parsnip's grey flannel shorts and hide them behind the toilet.'

And so they did.

And when the rest of my class had changed back into their school uniforms, there was I, searching the locker room in my baggy *Man from U.N.C.L.E.* underpants.

Hilarious – for them. Humiliating for me. Especially when I entered the classroom in my pants, gulping back the tears and holding a trembling hand in the air. 'Please, miss,' I gulped. 'I can't find my trousers . . .'

How they roared. I remember every excruciating second. The glee on their faces, the choked-up feeling in my throat. And it was my first experience of that brutal, shameful, cheek-burning, eye-stinging dip in self-esteem that makes you wish you had never been born – or been born, but never lost your trousers.

It would be nice to think that we outgrow the world's ability to humiliate us. It would be comforting to think that when we leave schoolbooks and playgrounds behind, we say good riddance to all that. And then one day – decades after the vicious japes of childhood are past – the terrible truth sinks in.

Someone is always hiding your trousers.

How can a grown man be humiliated? Losing something you were planning on keeping – your wife, your job, your underwear – these are the classics.

In the personal realm, being dumped by a woman you love immediately makes you feel as though you are five years old and some snickering bastard just stashed your short trousers in a secret hiding place. In the professional realm, losing your job is an infallible shortcut to humiliation.

Those two million unemployed will one day forget the sickening practicalities of unemployment – struggling to pay the bills, and confronting a cashpoint machine that has learned to say no. But they will never ever forget the feeling of not being wanted. They will never shake off the shame of being surplus to requirements. Bills get paid and bruises fade. A good woman can be replaced by a better woman. But the sting of humiliation stays with you forever.

Yet we are so ill equipped to deal with it. Humiliation – the ability of the wicked world to steal our trousers – always seems to sneak up on us.

The hard knocks of the working world, the fickle nature of

romance, even the subtle betrayals of our body as we age –
we see all these coming over the horizon and slowly marching
towards us. But humiliation always feels box fresh.

At the end of an American book tour I sat in a radio station
in California listening to the most loving introduction I had ever
heard in my life. 'Tonight,' said the DJ, 'we have a man in the
studio whose work has touched the lives and the hearts of literally millions . . . a man who is just a man and yet – through
the power of his work – unlike other men . . . Yes,' he said,
'Michael Douglas is coming into the studio later. But first . . .
someone called Tommy Perkins.'

The cliché of the American book tour is that they have not
read your book. The humiliating reality is that they rarely know
you have written a book. From sea to shining sea, I have had
hundreds of witless, white-toothed morons in assorted American
radio and TV stations ask me, 'What's the item?'

They usually ask you about ten seconds before you are live
on air. It means – Why are you here, dirt bag? And exactly
why were you born?

You may fret about the night you could not get an erection,
or that unfortunate flirtation with premature ejaculation, or when
your mum caught you masturbating over the bra ad in her
Littlewoods catalogue – especially if it was all on the same day
– but you have not really taken a masterclass in humiliation
until you have been on an American book tour.

I once did an event in Boston where, in the middle of a
crowded, bustling book shop, I faced row upon row of empty

seats. Only two people came – and one of them was a homeless person who woke up the moment I started speaking and
spent the rest of the event trying to sneak out without hurting
my feelings. It was very thoughtful of him. But it was far too
late. This was gold-medal humiliation – mortification as an
Olympic sport.

And I was humiliated again when only one woman turned
up in Dallas. And I was humiliated when the only books I shifted
in Atlanta were the dozen or so that were stolen by the same
smiling young man. And I was humiliated in Chicago when the
only question from the audience was from a mental little old
lady who was obsessed with the British Royal Family.

'Do you know Prince Philip?'

'No, unfortunately I have never met the Duke of Edinburgh.
Anyone else? Yes, the same lady . . .'

'How about Prince Charles?'

And so it went on – from the next in line to the throne all
the way down to the Duchess of Devonshire. And it was . . .
humiliating.

But not quite as bad as being eleven years old, and realising that there was a girl in my class that I wanted to spend
the rest of my life with.

Far too shy to actually talk to her, I cunningly waited
until Valentine's Day and then left a soppy, heart-covered
card on her desk, with my name written in big black letters.
And when I walked into the classroom on the morning of
14th February, there she was, holding my card, surrounded

by her friends – and my friends too! – and they were all wetting their regulation school knickers, pointing at me and laughing themselves sick.

From the womb to the tomb, from the cradle to the grave, the humiliation just keeps on coming. And it often kicks you right in your wedding tackle just when you were starting to think that you have the hang of this life thing.

Humiliation is life's way of telling you that, somewhere deep down inside, you will always be that scared little boy who couldn't find his trousers, or who was so naïve that he gave his Valentine card to the class heartbreaker, or made the terrible error of not being Michael Douglas when he was passing through California.

You think you grow out of being humiliated, but you never do. The job goes. Or the woman. Or perhaps you keep the job and the woman but somehow misplace your dignity – and that can hurt as much as all the rest.

TV is ripe for humiliation. I have seen people go on *Question Time* and shake so much that I hid behind the sofa. And I have seen people appear on *Have I Got News for You* and be so terrified that they never managed to say a full sentence – let alone exchange cutting, Oscar Wilde-level banter with the regular presenters. And then there was the poor sap who went on *Mastermind* and only managed to get two questions right in his specialist subject. How the world howled at his humiliation! The *Daily Mail* had a double-page spread on the humiliated thicko – AND YOUR SPECIALIST SUBJECT IS . . . PASS!!

I have done my unremarkable stints on *Question Time* and *Have I Got News for You* and *Mastermind*. And every time I left the studio I heaved an enormous sigh of relief. Because – while I had hardly set the world on fire with my wit, or intelligence, or knowledge – I had managed to avoid being totally humiliated.

And yet it comes to us all. It doesn't really matter if you never know the horror of the American book tour or finding yourself unable to stop shaking on *Question Time*. Life will humiliate you elsewhere. Humiliation is wonderfully democratic like that.

I remember the first public speech I ever made. Those who know me as an accomplished after-dinner speaker, always equipped with a stream of gags and an amusing jar of cock rub, would have been shocked to see my total humiliation on my debut speaking engagement.

It was the last century. George Michael was twenty-four years old and so naturally it was time to write his life story. George and I were doing the book together. He talked and I tarted it up. Our publishers threw a big party for us at the Groucho Club. And I was asked to give the keynote speech. And it was one of the most humiliating experiences of my life. Because my speech stunk the place out.

I did not realise at the time that you can't just write a speech and then read it out loud. I didn't realise that if you do that then every single time you look up, you completely lose your place. And have to find it again. And then you stutter, and sweat, and feel like crying as George Michael and all these publishing big shots look at you but can't meet your eye, just in case humiliation is contagious.

These days, I can speak in public until the audience soaks their Tiramisu with tears of mirth. And if we are ever in a changing room together, don't even think about hiding my trousers because I never let them out of my sight.

But so what? Life will find some other way to humiliate me. We all get humiliated. The question is – what are you going to do about it?

Humiliation can be a springboard to greatness. When Muhammad Ali fought Joe Frazier in Madison Square Garden on 8th March 1971 they were both undefeated, and those of us who had grown up watching Ali firmly believed him to be unbeatable. Ali no doubt believed it too.

But Smoking Joe not only beat Ali – he broke his jaw. Joe quite literally shut Ali's big, mocking mouth – the mouth that never tired of talking about how ugly Frazier was, and what an Uncle Tom he was, and what an inferior black man (despite Frazier's skin being far darker than Ali's). Ali was abjectly humiliated in Madison Square Garden that night. And yet somehow his greatness springs from that moment.

'Everybody loses,' he said thoughtfully. 'Probably be a better man.'

And so it proved.

And as Ali digested the humiliation of his first defeat, his face broken and swollen, those of us who loved him had never loved him more. Because he faced down humiliation like a man.

Frank Sinatra was the official photographer for *Life* magazine at that fight because he could not get a ringside seat. You might think that would be demeaning for one of the biggest stars in the world, but Sinatra's legend is built on the way he dealt with humiliation after early success.

Before Sinatra landed two contracts – to play Private Maggio in *From Here to Eternity*, and a recording contract with Capitol records – he was all washed up. What we think of when we think of Sinatra – the concept albums with Nelson Riddle, the Oscar-winning acting – only came after the world had humiliated him. In 1952, after being dropped by Columbia and MCA, Frank Sinatra did not even have a recording contract. Humiliation indeed – but greatness was just two contracts away.

It would be comforting to believe that humiliation is invariably the gateway to glory. Unfortunately, losing your trousers – literally or metaphorically – is rarely the cue for winning an Oscar, or beating Smoking Joe in Manila. Despite all the humiliations that life brings, true greatness eludes us. But deep down inside the lowest moments of all is where you know yourself at last.

It never really ends. If childhood is ripe for humiliation, then so is puberty. And young manhood is stuffed with humiliating moments – losing a fight I remember as being particularly humiliating. It might not have been the Thriller in Manila, but it mattered desperately to me. Yet being beaten physically is nothing to the damage you receive psychologically. Sticks and head butts can break your bones, but it is the abject humiliation that really hurts.

What must old age be like? An endless series of doctors peering up your back passage and asking you to cough and telling you to put your trousers back on.

But you can't!

Because the doctor has hidden them!

Seven

Tough Guys
Get Facials

In the never-ending battle to be the best a man can be, the twenty-first century male is confronted by the same question again and again – where to draw the line?

Laser surgery to correct imperfect eyesight, cosmetic dentistry to give you a perfect smile – this is now the kind of routine self-improvement that we get done in our lunch break. But – where does it end? Or doesn't it?

Over the last year I have had two red-blooded heterosexual males inform me that they plan to invest in a bottom-lift – which is exactly the same as a face-lift, but south of the border, down Mexico way. And to me – sorry – that just feels like a self-improvement too far.

Yet there is no denying that men are missing out on a lot of the things that women take for granted, and that make them healthier, happier and lovelier. And don't men have the right to be healthier, happier and lovelier too?

What about the facial? To many men – for example, me – the

facial has always been on the dark side of what is acceptable for a man. A bit too poncy. A tad too girly. Which just goes to show how far men still have to go.

Your dad and uncles would have reacted to a man-facial with distrust. Well, I have been to the mountain, and I have had a facial – and I see at last what I have been missing for years.

This just in – real men get facials.

As fallible, neurotic, profoundly messed-up human beings, we all have an insatiable appetite for self-improvement.

Or is that just me?

I am shocked and disturbed to discover that for every Penguin Classic or slim volume of poetry on my shelves, I seem to own many more books on getting rich, getting laid, getting fit, losing weight, winning fights, raising daughters, stopping smoking, starting a language and treating your own knees. I am a sucker for self-improvement, a junkie for self-help, a crack whore of self-motivation.

Or is that just my library?

But everywhere I look there is evidence of a pathological obsession for being richer, tougher, thinner, smarter, fitter and – above all – better.

There are books by world-renowned experts here. Captain W.E. Fairbairn's 1942 martial arts classic *Get Tough! How to win in hand-to-hand fighting as taught to the British commandos and the U.S Armed Forces.* And oh look – there is the babe-magnet bible, *How to Get the Women You Desire into Bed* by sex guru Ross Jeffries. And right next to it I see *How to Get Rich* by Donald Trump. There's *The Prince* by Machiavelli and Sun Tzu's *The Art of War*, books about Neuro-Linguistic Programming and Creative Visualisation and how to end a street fight with just one blow.

But do I really need this stuff? And has it done me any good? Does it do anyone any good?

Not all the self-improvement texts I own are by some certified genius in his field. I also have a large collection of books by charlatans, nutjobs and nobodies. I own books about getting rich by people who are not rich but in jail. But when it comes to improving myself, I seem disturbingly willing to suspend belief. I am like a country hick queuing up to see the bearded lady, the mug punter who can't see when the cards are marked, a sucker for that snake oil.

I am even starting to doubt the experts. Captain W.E. Fairbairn invented the Fairbairn Commando knife and is the father of modern hand-to-hand combat. Anyone with fire in the blood should own a copy of *Get Tough!* But Fairbairn takes an entire chapter to tell you how to tie a German soldier to a tree – *with his own legs.* Even if I learn how to do it really, really well, how often is that going to come in useful to me?

And as much as I admire Donald Trump, can I really learn the secrets of his success in chapters entitled 'Bullshit Will Only Get You So Far' and 'Look Closely Before Changing Careers' and 'Think Big and Live Large'. As with most maharishis of motivation you sense that Trump can't explain the secret of his success because he doesn't really know it himself. The most interesting pearl of wisdom is Trump's revelation that, while most big-swinging dicks believe in a firm handshake, he personally believes in no handshake at all.

Interesting. Very interesting. But if I drop the handshakes I fear that people will just think I am a weirdo. I doubt that it will make me as rich as The Donald.

So it is with Ross Jeffries. The godfather of modern seduction has channelled a number of disciplines – Neuro-Linguistic Programming, hypnotherapy, wearing silky bathrobes – into the black art of picking up girls. But when he comes out with a line like, DON'T PLACE A PERSONAL AD! I can't help thinking to myself – gee, Ross, what kind of feverishly masturbating losers do you think you are talking to here?

I admire Ross Jeffries (for turning seduction into a philosophy), just as I admire Donald Trump (for losing his fortune and then making another), and Captain Fairbairn (for showing my father how to tie up a Nazi with his own legs). But will their books really make me a better man? We crave change, and yet somehow change never comes.

Until you have your first facial.

'The face is not another planet,' says Su-Man Hsu. 'Even men who are very fit, even men who are fanatics about going to the gym, even men who care very much about the state of their bodies – even these men tend to neglect their faces.'

Here the London-based Taiwanese health guru shoots me one of her legendary dirty looks.

'As though the face is somehow separate from the rest of the body,' she says. 'And it is not. And it never will be. But the reason why most facials in the world are ineffectual rubbish – even the facials you will get at five-star spas – is because they treat the face as separate from everything else. The fools!'

Su-Man Hsu is a body therapist with a client base so A-list that you feel a little self-conscious about going to see her if you have never won an Oscar.

Indeed, having an Academy Award on your mantelpiece is no guarantee that she will be able to fit you in. During a recent visit to London, Nicole Kidman called three times and still couldn't be squeezed in. Sorry, Nicole. Su-Man's diary is pretty full.

Nicole Kidman got a knockback because Su-Man was too busy whipping a certain Oscar-winning French actress into shape. But she would have got a knockback even if Su-Man had been fully booked with the high-end housewives and investment bankers who also comprise her client list. She is fanatically loyal to her clients, and they remain devoted to her. Even post-Crunch, she is big in the City.

When you see an investment banker jump off a roof, Su-Man Hsu is probably the reason his skin looks so good.

Juliette Binoche, the late Anthony Minghella, James Bond

director Marc Foster, *Harry Potter* producer David Heyman –
they all take off their shoes and check their egos at the door
when they come to Su-Man's spa (a beautiful converted summerhouse in the back garden of her London home).

'The reason that most facials are useless is because they
don't even massage the shoulders and neck muscles,' Su-Man
says, as I rip off my shirt. 'And the shoulders and neck muscles
are why a face sags as it gets older.'

What's she looking at me for?

A lot of the self-improvement industry promises 'shortcuts to
success'. Shortcuts to the richer, tougher, fitter man that we all
want to be. This is especially true in the money end of the market
– perhaps because we want to gain untold riches more than we
want to lose those few extra pounds, or master the elbow strike
to the temple. But of course there are no shortcuts to anything
worth having. Whether you are losing weight or learning martial
arts or building a property empire worth billions, you do not do
it in ten easy steps. It takes a lifetime, not a lunchtime.

And yet, and yet . . . we just can't help believing that it
is possible to learn the wisdom of the ancients in a £9.99
paperback.

The belief that we can gather the information needed to
radically improve ourselves is the kryptonite of the men of today.
And even those who would sneer at the cosy banalities of a
non-book like *Who Moved My Cheese? An amazing way to*

deal with change in your work and in your life (the one with the mouse who gave up, and the mouse who didn't) are likely to quote knowingly from Machiavelli's *The Prince* or, the grand-daddy of them all, Sun Tzu's *The Art of War*.

The Prince, the defining text of realpolitik, was written five centuries ago. *The Art of War,* the most famous book ever written about military tactics, was written more than two thousand years ago. But we do not read Machiavelli or Sun Tzu because they wrote wise, gripping narratives about human beings struggling for survival and victory long ago and far away. We read them because we genuinely believe that they have practical things to tell us about our life and work now. We read Sun Tzu because we think he will be able to help us when we have a falling out with Doris from Accounts. We read Machiavelli because we think he has something relevant to say about the bloke at the next desk getting promoted ahead of you.

The Art of War and *The Prince* are historical artefacts, but they are published, sold and read as lessons in business strategy. Sun Tzu became the guru of every middle manager from Sydney to San Francisco when it was revealed that Mike Ovitz, legendary Hollywood agent, had a copy of *The Art of War* by his bedside. But did Sun Tzu ever really help Ovitz? Maybe. Although when you read a Sun Tzu line such as, 'With regards to narrow passes, if you can occupy them first, let them be strongly garrisoned and await the advent of the enemy,' it is difficult to see how much practical help it could possibly be when Ovitz was negotiating Sharon Stone's residuals on *Basic Instinct.*

And yet we can't resist the illusion of learning *what gifted people know.* How could I ever feel that I don't need *How to Be Rich* by J. Paul Getty? How could I *not* buy a book called *Only Fat People Skip Breakfast?* What man or boy doesn't have a well-thumbed copy of *Hef's Little Black Book* by Hugh Hefner? Or at least a copy that you open once and then toss aside at the mind-numbing obviousness of it all. I mean, all due respect to the man with the pipe, but do I really need advice from Hef on 'How to look at a nude photograph'? If I can't work that out by myself . . . shoot me, Hef.

Many of the masters of seduction end up unintentionally insulting you. Just as I recoil with revulsion when Ross Jeffries starts talking about personal ads, and get the sinking feeling that his sex handbook is actually aimed at other, lesser men, so Hefner's thoughts on Viagra are like being hit in the trousers with a wet fish. 'If you take Viagra one hour before the fact, it can last eight to twelve hours. There's always a time when you're looking for wood – nights when you've been drinking a lot, for example – and it may not be there. It provides the certainty that wood is there when you need it.'

Viagra? Not for at least another six months, Hef. The wood is still there when needed. Hefner, like all the other scholars of self-improvement, ultimately leaves me feeling cheated.

Because I do not want the odd helpful tip. Or even lots of un-helpful tips. I want transformation, revelation and secrets revealed.

I want to know how to be *much* richer, *much* tougher, *much* thinner. If I want a few titbits of helpful information, then I will buy *The Good Food Guide*. I want a Big Bang that changes everything, I want a brand-new me.

If you really want to impress me – promise me a new face.

'I don't just give you a facial,' Su-Man Hsu says. 'It is not just about cleaning pores, exfoliating dead skin and toning. It is about exercising the face. If a facial doesn't do that – then don't bother.'

I get on the couch and throw myself at her mercy. And if not sixty minutes of gentle but ultimately worthless stroking, then what should you expect from a facial by Su-Man Hsu?

'You should look healthier,' she says. 'Happier. More confident. And there should be a glow that wasn't there before.' Then she gets that cheeky grin that somehow makes her bossy manner bearable. She is like the good cop and bad cop all in one authoritative package.

'Like George Clooney – but better.'

Su-Man Hsu's background is dance. She spent a year on the road with Juliette Binoche and Akram Khan in the National Theatre co-production *in-i* (she taught Binoche to dance for the role – no easy task, as anyone who caught *in-i* will testify).

Su-Man was a ballet dancer in her native Taiwan, and later joined the European dance company Rosas. A back injury at the age of twenty introduced her to the healing properties of shiatsu massage – an applied pressure massage that is a lot like acupuncture without the needles.

Shiatsu is all about loosening up your tired old body and increasing the flow of *chi* – the life energy that flows through us all. How to explain the Chinese concept of *chi*? Well, *chi* is just like the Force in *Star Wars*, except it is real. A therapist who understands *chi* can see serious disease coming over the horizon. Su-Man knew her friend and client Anthony Minghella was unwell before he did.

Su-Man teaches Hollywood superstars to dance (that's why Nicole Kidman was calling), she uses hard-core sweat-your-nuts-off Pilates to keep those A-listers trim, shiatsu massage to keep them loose and her own special total-body facials to keep them lovely.

But to her it is all one thing. And the good news is that it works. Which is why those Hollywood big shots keep coming back for more.

The facial is, quite frankly, seventy-five minutes of pleasure and pain. The soothing, chilled-out bliss of having a master therapist devote her time to only you – and sort out a few medical problems on the way (she made me realise that my neck had been aching for months). And the pain of having someone manipulate the muscles in your face until they are vaguely where they should be.

Whatever you do with Su-Man – from the facial to Pilates to Shiatsu to learning to dance – it is not for wimps or the weak-hearted. Along with the deep-cleansing moisturiser, expect agony and ecstasy. A BBC documentary on Juliette Binoche learning to dance with Su-Man for their show, revealed that the French minx was covered in bruises. Binoche did not look as though she was learning to dance. She looked as if she had just played ninety minutes against Don Revie's Leeds United. But back to that facial . . .

First Su-Man assesses the state of your skin, and then cleans your face while a steam machine gently opens your filthy pores. Soon the summerhouse is filled with more smoke than the video for 'Bohemian Rhapsody'.

Next comes some serious exfoliating – the removal of dead skin – and then the stuff that makes her unique. She gets her fingers and thumbs stuck into the muscles of your shoulders and neck, and manipulates away the damage of the years. Not an easy task. But the physical power of the woman!

When I whimper with pain, she tells me that this is the crucial bit – the kind of thing they will not do for you in those scented spas at your holiday hotel – but this is the very essence of her facial. The massage and stimulation of face muscles, to shake off the depressing droopiness that comes with the passing of the years.

But – oh, mother – the pain.

'Nothing ages a man like the sagging of his jaw,' she says. 'So stop whining.'

Su-Man applies a clear collagen mask over my entire face, including my eyes. No need to panic! This is deep, penetrating hydration, so that my skin loses some of that dried-out prune-featured look that Kate Moss has made so fashionable.

'The years and unhealthy living remove the moisture from your skin,' Su-Man says. 'So we have to put it back.'

I have never had a facial before – what kind of sissy boy do you think I am? – but I imagine that a lot of what Su-Man does – the cleaning of pores, the exfoliating, the hydration – is what you would expect from any superior facial. What is different about Su-Man is her holistic, Chinese approach – the creed that a facial is only one part of full-body therapy. I stumbled in with a bad cold, and when I complain that my nose is completely blocked, she briskly massages the bottom of my eye sockets . . . and my nasal passages are suddenly clear. They will not do that for you at the spa in the Four Seasons. This is what I love about the woman – she knows how to fix you.

Again and again, she comes back to the line about the face not being another planet, and while my collagen mask is replenishing my skin, Su-Man demonstrates her code by massaging the muscles in my legs, and attempting to pull my toes off.

After the collagen mask comes off, I get more massage in the shoulders and neck. It feels great – like being an old tom cat that is being stroked after a night on the tiles. But was my face really so saggy? Oh yes – and this is the almost indefinable quality that puts years on your clock. The way gravity pulls you down as the summers die one by one.

'Juliette Binoche was the face of Lancôme for years,'

Su-Man says. 'But it wasn't their products that made her look like that. It was me.'

I believe her. After a morning with Su-Man, I feel that I will soon be ready to model skin products for Lancôme myself.

Su-Man applies a second mask of Vitamin E – a soothing, deep-tissue hydration to give me the glow that the ladies love. While that is setting like stone over my eyes – it is not quite as totally terrifying as it sounds – Su-Man massages my arms, hands and scalp.

There is something brutally soothing about being massaged by the hands of Su-Man. Even when you suffer, you feel that it will all be worth it. In the end. When the mask is removed I am given a final moisturising massage before we end with what is known as the percussion technique – which is basically being smacked in the face, and having your head treated like a set of bongos that need to be broken in.

And when I look in the mirror . . . it has worked. Somehow – after seventy-five minutes of intensive care – my skin has lost that dry, papery look that I had resigned myself to. I don't look anywhere near so shagged out and tired. I don't look so old. I am glowing like the first light of a summer dawn. My face looks less like the Dead Sea scrolls and more like a newly minted first edition.

And if I am not quite George Clooney – hey, the woman can't perform miracles – then I am certainly not quite as baggy, saggy and George Michael-like as I was before. But my face is only a part of it.

My legs, my arms, my neck, my shoulders, my feet – they all feel looser than they have in years. My blood seems to be pumping again. I don't ache in the places where I used to play. I want to do it again. It's a lot like childbirth – you forget the pain and remember the pleasure.

And I feel better. And I feel good. But then that is what Su-Man Hsu does – you give her a hundred quid and she makes you feel like a million euros.

Which is why all those people with stiff limbs, dry skin and Oscars are standing outside her door. And they still can't get in.

At first glance, the self-improvement industry seems to represent all our basest instincts. It is hard not to contemplate books with titles like *How to Get Rich* and *How to Win Dirty* and *How to Get Beautiful Women Even if You Are a Really Ugly Bastard* and not believe that they are manifestations of all inside us that is greedy, gluttonous and venal.

But perhaps that is too hard, for we all want to be better men, and our constant seeking for paths to improvement is a natural and healthy instinct. It's just that the road to Nirvana is paved with many dead ends and wrong turnings and useless books with titles like *Millionaire Upgrade*.

The books that have helped me most have all been how-to books for writers. *The Writer's Journey* by Christopher Vogler. *The War of Art* by Steven Pressfield. *Story* by Robert McKee.

But I came to them all with a specific problem, or set of problems, when I was stuck mid-book, and they helped me to fix it.
They are not bibles but instruction booklets. I took only what I
needed and had no expectations that they would give me wings.
It is the difference between wanting to know how to change a
tyre and wanting to know how to change your life. The second
one takes a little longer.

For there are never easy answers. There's no such thing as
a quick fix. The terrible truth is that Sun Tzu and Machiavelli
actually can't help you with Doris in Accounts. *Only Fat People
Skip Breakfast* will not stop you being a chubby chops if you
do not conquer your oral fixation. Reading *The Richest Man in
Babylon* by George S. Clason will not clear your overdraft.
Reading Captain W. E. Fairbairn's *Get Tough!* will probably
not do you much good in a pub fight. The road to being a
better man is long and hard and lashed with many stones, and
we must all walk it alone.

In Herman Hesse's *Siddhartha*, a novel about the spiritual
evolution of a young man living in India at the time of the
Buddha, the young monk has to immerse himself in every experience before he can reach enlightenment. In *Groundhog
Day*, the Bill Murray character has to be reborn every morning
and travel through despair, nihilism, hedonism, compassion,
love and death itself before he can achieve a state of grace.

How long does it take? Danny Rubin, the writer of *Groundhog
Day*, has said he thought his character was reborn every day
for ten years – 'long enough to learn how to play the piano'.

Harold Ramis, the film's director, has said that he thought the Bill Murray character was reborn for ten thousand years. We know in our hearts that it will take a lifetime to be the person we want to be. And then some.

We crave perfection, enlightenment, and an end to all cares – physical, financial, sexual, emotional, spiritual. When I buy a book promising to reveal the shortcut to apocalyptic sex, a six-pack and the Rich List, I know I am wasting my time. I know in my heart that I can learn more from one page of Graham Greene than I can from an entire shelf of books promising to make me richer, tougher or thinner.

But I also know that our desire to be far more than we are is what dragged us from the trees, and what makes us get out of bed every morning, and what drives us on every day and what may yet lead us to glory.

We crave richer. We crave tougher. We crave peace of mind. Even when the smart move would be counting our blessings. To stop fretting that we do not look like the men in the glossy ads. To stop worrying that we are faulty versions of all we should be. To start feeling pride in who we are, and stop feeling all this shame for all that we are not.

And when we have done all that, we should book a facial.

Eight

You Only Wed Twice

I was single for ten years between my first marriage and my second marriage – which gives you some idea of how much I enjoyed my first marriage.

Or maybe it doesn't. Maybe those ten years of the single life say nothing about being married but plenty about the brutal business of getting divorced.

Because after a decade of married women, German au pairs and assorted crazy chicks – oh, come on, you know the routine – after ten years of multiple partners, strange beds and the loneliness of the twenty-four-hour party people, I was ready to give marriage another shot.

I believed I knew why the marriage to Julie had failed, and why the marriage to Yuriko would work. And I missed being married. Craved it like crazy, to be honest. Like all men, even during the happy times of the single life, I secretly yearned for a successful marriage. Being happily married somehow seemed like a big step up from being single – even happily single.

So do I believe that men want to get married as much as women? Do I believe that spraying your oats around the hotels of five continents is ultimately no substitute for a stable, loving home and a partner for life?

Do I seriously believe that – no matter how loudly we protest – men want a successful marriage as much as any chick-lit heroine?

I do.

The average length of a marriage in these islands is eleven years and six months. So the average marriage – the marriage all the statistics suggest you can reasonably expect – will self-destruct before any children produced by that union reach puberty.

And that's not a marriage from hell.

That is normal.

But nobody ever got married thinking, Oh well, with good behaviour I will be out after eleven years and six months. The thing about getting married, especially for the first time, is that you never doubt that it will last forever. And that cocky certainty does for more marriages than eyeing the bridesmaids with a wicked glint in your eye.

When you do it for the second time, you take greater care – in everything. Your choice of partner, your resistance to – as the Squeeze song says – the fruits of another. And by now you know that if your marital home is marred by petty domestic squabbles, then you are most certainly in the wrong marital home. Try next door.

And as the suppurating wounds of your first marriage heal, you learn to cut that aborted union some slack. I always felt bewildered when people told me that my first marriage 'failed'. Says who?

We had seven years together, five of them as husband and wife, most of them happy, at a time in our lives when we were both basically a couple of crazy kids. Not bad going. The marriage produced a wonderful child – and who has the right to say that any marriage that produces a wonderful child has failed? Maybe it just ran its course.

I know of plenty of failed marriages where the husband and wife stayed together.

I look at my first marriage and I know why it fell apart. I look at my second marriage and I know why it has lasted. Julie was a friend who became a lover who became my wife. We were young. When we got married I was twenty-five and Julie was even younger. Our friends were still boys and girls about town. But marriage seemed like an inevitable step for us. Especially when we learned we were to become parents.

There were good times. We loved our baby. But we were so young, we were so chronically poor and we had absolutely no idea how tough life – and marriage – can be. It was as if we were a couple of big kids, playing at grown-ups. Money problems weighed on our marriage like migraine, like a ton of red bills. Extreme youth did too. We sought escape in the beds of other people. I can't speak for my ex-wife, but I had no idea that infidelity kills a marriage stone dead. Then I found out.

Divorce was more than mere heartbreak. It was an education. I had broken up with plenty of girls before, but this experience was light years away from the trauma of adolescent heartache.

No, it turned out that we weren't kids after all – not with a child of our own and a marriage certificate and a broken home. It wasn't like splitting up with a girlfriend. We were *married*. Until a judge signed a piece of paper, and suddenly we weren't. What was I meant to do with my wedding ring? What did you do with all the photographs? What did you do with the rest of your life?

I didn't have a clue.

Our son Bobby was four years old and he stayed with me – unusual, but Julie was busy with her new life, her new family – and pregnant with the new guy's baby. Our marriage was not just over, it was dead and buried and a thorn in our souls. We both made an attempt to remain civilised for the sake of our son, but that didn't last long. There was bitterness on both sides and we were hurtful and hateful to each other. For years and years and years. Bystanders rubbed their hands with glee. Our son – this beautiful four-year-old boy who had done nothing wrong – was caught in the crossfire. We forgot all we had shared. We showed no mercy. We were cruel and dumb.

Still in my twenties, I was a divorced man and a single parent. And I railed at how stupid I had been. Stupid to get married when I was so young, so poor, still struggling to get my career going. And so careless to choose Julie as my wife. But that's a big problem with all first marriages – you basically get stuck with the first person that you can talk to all night long.

Marriage simply didn't come up for most of my thirties. I was like one of those Hugh Grant characters – a commitment-phobe, reluctant to put down my emotional anchor, scared witless of caring too much and then getting hurt. I met armies of women, and dozens of them would have been a better choice of wife than Julie, who should have been a summer romance, or possibly dinner and a movie. But when they mentioned marriage, I headed for the exit door and I didn't look back.

Golly gosh, Matron! Oh, I say! The big difference between Hugh Grant and me is that I had a little boy. I was a single man, and a single parent too. Marriage? I had been there, done that, and got the shrapnel wounds. Then I met Yuriko. And I knew before the end of our first conversation that I wanted to marry her, and have a baby with her, and see her face before me when I drew my dying breath. She was beautiful, funny, kind, smart – just endlessly likeable, and endlessly love-able. And by now I had met a lot of women. I was no longer a young man in my twenties, walking down the aisle although he knew nothing of life, nothing of love. I was a man in my thirties who had been through the divorce courts. I looked at Yuriko and all the cynicism and bitterness in me seemed to melt away like teardrops in the rain. Lightning struck, and when that happens you have found the woman you should marry.

Despite the feeling Yuriko effortlessly inspired in me – and the feeling was love – I was also able to look at our relationship with a clear-eyed pragmatism that only comes when you have a broken marriage behind you.

We got on. We clicked. Yes, we loved each other. Yet there was something more – I believed that, if we got married, then it would work. We could be happy. We would stick together. We would survive the tough times. The odds were in our favour. But this time I knew what I would have to do to make it work.

My second marriage (Yuriko's first) was a white wedding in a big church. The first, to Julie, had been in a registry office, the bride clearly and massively pregnant, with a honeymoon of bacon sandwiches in a dingy flat. Very traditional.

What made my second marriage work? On a practical level, I am simply not the wild young twenty-something with empty pockets that I was in my first marriage. I am calmer, more settled in my skin and in my career. There are no red bills falling through the door on a daily basis. I have kissed my fair share of women – and perhaps somebody else's share too.

And all that helps. But choosing the right person, and understanding how you build a life together, that helps even more. Then you have a child and this baby grows into the most special person you have ever met, and that makes the marriage feel like it is set in stone.

So far, so good. And I think that if any marriage is going

to work – be it your first, second or tenth – then that is what you need to say every day of your life.

So far, so good.

Marriage is good for men. Research at the University of Arizona, published in the *Psychosomatic Medicine* journal, claims that married men are less prone to heart disease, depression and stroke than their single brothers because married men have lower levels of CRP in their bloodstream – the C-reactive protein, produced by the liver in response to inflammation and responsible for all manner of nastiness. Some academics go even further, suggesting that marriage is better for men than giving up smoking.

Men respond to the stability that marriage brings, and even when it all goes horribly wrong, we eventually feel like giving it another try. Now more than ever – although marriage is a declining institution, the recession has seen a spike in the marriage figures. All over the country registry offices and churches report a strong surge in marriages since the economic collapse of autumn 2008. In uncertain times we hunger for the certainties of marriage – or at least what we kid ourselves are the certainties of marriage.

And yet, in good times or bad, there is a part of the male soul that holds back from the loving arms of marriage.

There is a part of us that thinks – yeah but no but. There are so many fabulous women in the world, so why choose just one fabulous woman? We hear the call of Neverland, we dream of a life of magic and adventure. The call of the wild. The siren song of married women, German au pairs and crazy chicks. Always there is this lingering pining for the single life.

In 1980, on the eve of his sixth marriage, Norman Mailer fell into a deep depression. 'Norman,' said Norris, his beautiful bride-to-be, 'on the eve of our wedding day, what troubles you so?'

Mailer took a breath and spilled his guts out. He never wanted all these marriages, he said. He never wanted all these divorces. All he ever wanted . . . *was to be a free man in Paris.*

And Norris took his hand and spelled it out. If Mailer was a free man in Paris, he would go to a restaurant, and he would see some heartbreaking young beauty, and he would fall heavily – and they would end up married. And he saw that it was true. And so Norman Mailer married Norris the next day, and they stayed married until his dying day, twenty-seven years later.

And if marriage ever dies out, it will not be because of bruised old romantics like me and Norman Mailer. No, it will be because of our children – all those products of broken homes who understand better than anyone the fragility of marriage, and the devastating fallout when it all comes apart. Adults eventually get over a broken marriage. But children never do.

Get married? Why would they want to do a crazy thing like that? They have already been through one divorce.

And one divorce is plenty.

Nine

Getting Tested

I went to see my doctor with a sore elbow and he told me that he wanted to test me for cancer.

Don't you just hate it when that happens?

I pointed out to my doc that I was there because I live a robust, sporty, healthy lifestyle. I wasn't pissing blood. My elbow hurt because I am so healthy. Didn't that exempt me from cancer tests? Couldn't I be excused?

But the doctor was insistent – although low key with it, and almost apologetic. I was there on the GP's couch already. It wouldn't take a minute. He didn't say it, but we both thought it – *what was I afraid of?*

Oh, you know – terminal illness, premature death, abandonment of wife and child, a tumour as big as the Ritz. All the usual stuff.

We shared a moment of manly embarrassment, my doctor and I. He wanted to test me – for my own good. And I didn't even want to think about it. Thanks but no thanks.

'But it's good to know, isn't it?' said the doctor.

Is it? Is it really good to know? I would have thought it is

good to know if your body is a cancer-free zone. Is it quite
so good to know when you have a tumour the dimensions of
a grapefruit growing halfway up your rectum?

And the answer to that is – Yes, Tony. It's good to know
whether you are sick because if you can catch it early enough,
then you give yourself a fighting chance of beating it.

I know men like that. They are my friends. These brave,
beautiful men who have confronted cancer everywhere from
their bonce to their bollocks. And many places in between. And
they beat it. Because they caught it early. They gave themselves
a fighting chance.

Yeah, but still – I just didn't fancy it, to tell you the truth.
The whole knowing thing. And I didn't fancy being tested. I
didn't fancy the seven days or so wondering if my daughter
was going to grow up without a father. Most of all, I just didn't
want to think about it.

And that is what men are like. And this is when we are
confronted by what they call male stereotypical behaviour in
all its stubbornness, pride, bravery, cowardice and stupidity.

Getting tested.

'Men are dying of apathy, shame – and too much beer and
kebabs,' revealed the *Daily Mirror*.

Oh, well – it's better than being killed by a Nazi. Or is it?
The latest research is unequivocal: men are 40 per cent more
likely to die of cancer than women. A spokeswoman for Cancer

Research UK says, 'Far too many men are risking their lives by ignoring signs of cancer.'

The top five cancer-killers in men are pancreas (5 per cent), oesophagus (6 per cent), bowel (10 per cent), prostate (13 per cent) and lung cancer (24 per cent) at number one.

Lifestyle is a killer. The junk-food fix and empty calories of booze. But it is our he-man attitude to getting tested that really turns our behaviour suicidal.

It makes so much sense to get tested. Then why do we resist? Could it possibly be the thought of having another man stick his finger up our bottom?

'We don't do it like that any more,' said my doctor, with a flicker of distaste, as I pulled down my trousers and warily lifted my firm young buttocks into the air. 'Having someone rooting around in the dark with his index finger—' he shuddered '—it's very unscientific.'

Now you've disappointed me.

My doctor wanted to test me for prostate cancer – the second highest of cancer killers for men. That's where that famous slogan for prostate cancer comes from: *Number two, so we try harder.* Prostate cancer is the Avis of malignant tumours. But the way they test you for prostate cancer these days is with a PSA blood test.

A high level of PSA – prostate-specific antigen – can be a sign of cancer, or something else, like a urinary infection. The crucial bit is your PSA level. It goes up in increments of one every ten years or so, and is the ratio of nanograms of protein to millilitres of blood. So a healthy man under the age of forty would expect a PSA reading of around 2 or 3 ng/ml, while a robust old geezer over the age of seventy should expect a PSA reading of around 5 ng/ml. Your PSA will always be increasing throughout your life – but not by very much.

The scary bit is when you have a PSA blood test and it comes back not in low single digits but in the hundreds of thousands.

And basically what that would mean is – do you want to be buried or cremated?

I had the PSA blood test.

How could I refuse? God knows I tried.

The doctor was so full of common sense and compassion. And I was so full of, 'Is-that-really-the-time?' jibbering equivocation. In the end it would have been loony to walk out of there without getting tested.

He wouldn't let me be loony.

But I didn't like it. It wasn't the thought of prostate cancer – although, if you are a non-smoking man, it is statistically the kind of cancer most likely to claim you. It was having to think about it. It was having to admit that one day I will have something more serious than a sore elbow to worry about.

Although it was the smart thing to do, and the reasonable thing to do, and the only thing to do, getting tested still felt like letting the darkness into my life. The darkness of mortality, illness and hospital beds in cancer wards.

The funny thing is, I walked into that doctor's surgery knowing exactly what was wrong with me. Or at least I thought I did.

My trainer, Fred Kindall, had been wearing a particularly sturdy piece of body armour when I hit him with a right uppercut that badly jarred my wrist. So for the next few weeks, I boxed almost one-handed. Lots of stiff left jabs, left hooks, left upper-cuts. Overcompensating. Which is typical male stereotypical behaviour.

And it made my left elbow hurt.

'I've got tennis elbow,' I had confidently told the doc when I bowled into his surgery, almost telling him to take the rest of the day off. 'Lateral epicondylitis,' I added, effortlessly slipping into the Latin.

Men have always been prone to a bit of the old self-diagnosis. But the Internet has turned us all into first-year surgical interns. And of course I was wrong. 'No, what you have is *medial* epicondylitis,' corrected the doc. 'Golfer's elbow.'

Oh.

He explained that tennis elbow is the onset of pain and tenderness on the outside (lateral) part of the elbow, whereas golfer's elbow is the onset of pain and tenderness on the inside (medial) part of the elbow. What did I know? Nothing. Between you and me, I didn't even know that women don't have a prostate gland until he told me. I was stunned. This was news to me. We've got nipples but they don't have prostate glands? Is that right? It hardly seems fair.

When it comes to getting tested, male ignorance knows no bounds. Businessman David Hart wrote in the *Daily Telegraph* how he ignored the symptoms of his Motor Neurone Disease until he could ignore them no more. Then he went online with his symptoms – and diagnosed another condition entirely, something that he hadn't actually got. It was four years before he learned he had been suffering from Motor Neurone Disease all along. But then it is always easy to make a confident diagnosis of what ails us.

And so hard to confess that we always get it wrong.

Guess what? My PSA test came back and the result was *less than one.*

So what that basically means is my prostate gland is the Usain Bolt of prostate glands. It is Brad Pitt. It is Ronaldo. It is fit and fine. It is the promised gland. As prostate glands go, it is glowing with health. It is the gland of hope and glory. Yes, it's good to know. And I feel proud of the little fellow. The lad done good. My prostate gland can look to the future with optimism and confidence. It can hold its head up in any company. And I know one thing about my prostate gland.

It is going to be really upset if I get hit by a bendy bus.

*   *   *

We are told that it is time for male cancer to come out of the closet. That we need to be more like women, to stop seeing getting tested as a matter of life and death – although it is certainly that – and to do it as routine maintenance. Getting tested, from a female perspective, is not something you do because you are worried. It is just something you do, as a matter of course. And everyone agrees that men need to be more like that, and to stop seeing going to the doctor as silly girly nonsense.

And it is all true. When I read about the shocking death statistics of male cancer, and reflect that more men need to start getting tested more often, I can feel my prostate gland nodding solemnly in agreement. And yet, and yet . . . I can understand why men don't go. I can totally understand why there is this great male reluctance to get tested.

Prostate cancer kills around the same number of men every year as breast cancer kills women. And women fight back against that terrible disease – they get tested, they run marathons with their bras on top of their vests, they know all about it. Most men out there probably still think that getting tested for prostate cancer means an invasion of the Khyber Pass. I know I did.

Women don't understand us. They think we refuse to go to the doctor because it looks wimpy. That is not the case. Women – with their smear tests, and their examinations for breast cancer, and their awareness – do not look remotely wimpy to me. They look brave. But men have to be dragged kicking and screaming to get tested for one reason – it makes us feel less like men.

This is what they never get about male stereotypical behaviour. We need it. Not to the extent that we ignore a lump in our testicles, or a spot on our lungs. But we need it so that we can pretend that we are immortal.

We need a certain amount of that stubbornness, and that stupidity, just to get by, just to be who we are, just so we can be fully functioning male animals who can provide and protect the ones we love. We can't live our lives worried that the worst might happen. Why don't men go to the doctor more often? Because it would not be very manly.

Perhaps it is not too late. Perhaps we can learn to look the male cancer statistics in the eye and change just enough to still walk like a man while attempting to cancer-proof ourselves like women. Do it all. Live the dream. Provide, protect and sport a prostate gland that will make all the girls swoon.

But how about a bit of sympathy for male stereotypical behaviour?

Men are no keener to die of some awful kind of cancer than women. But getting tested comes about as naturally to us as putting on a dress. Better to die as a man than live with someone's finger up your bum. Even if it is only a metaphorical finger these days.

Getting tested makes us feel that we will not always be around to protect the people we love. It makes us admit that – for all the weight training, for all the cardio, for all the times you throw a big left hook at your own personal Fred – your body will weaken, and sicken, and eventually betray you. That is a hard thing for any man to accept. My hunch is that it's almost impossible.

There is something hardwired in us – something deep in our big-dick DNA, inseparable from those monstrous male chromosomes – that stops us getting tested at every possible opportunity.

It is not because we think we are immortal.

It is because, in the secret chambers of our heart, we know that we are not.

Ten

A Complicated Young God

English football is forever trapped in a moment, and returns to that moment endlessly, and can't get over it, and can't get enough of it, and broods about that moment as if it was a lost lover, seething with regret, wondering if the moment could ever come again.

Wembley Stadium, late in the afternoon of 30th July 1966. The sky is clear after summer rain. In their unfamiliar red shirts, the England team hoists their young captain on to their shoulders. In his right fist is the World Cup. On his face is a smile that lights up a decade, a sport, a nation.

Bobby Moore of West Ham United, twenty-five years old and in his triumphant prime, the England captain with the Jules Rimet trophy in one hand, and sunshine on his golden curls.

Bobby Moore would never again reach such heroic heights.

But then neither would England.

*   *   *

In the old photographs, it feels that you are always looking up at Bobby Moore. In the white shirt of England, in the claret and blue of West Ham, photographers tended to shoot Bobby from below, against a clear blue sky, to emphasise his heroic status.

But Bobby Moore – English football's ultimate hero – was a greater hero than we ever knew. Less than two years before England won the World Cup, at just twenty-three years of age, he was diagnosed with testicular cancer.

November 1964. Bobby Moore's heavily pregnant twenty-two-year-old wife Tina turns over in bed, suddenly pressing against him, and he wakes up, screaming in agony. 'You can't ignore it any longer,' his wife tells him. 'You have to see a doctor. You have to know.'

Until this moment, their life has been a dream. Earlier in the year, the Football Writers Association had voted him Footballer of the Year – the youngest ever to receive the honour. In May, in possibly the greatest FA Cup Final of all time, Moore led West Ham to victory over Preston, the Irons twice coming from behind and grabbing the winner in the dying seconds of injury time. Moore is the poster boy of English football. But suddenly everything is on the line. His career. His health. His life.

'Bobby had been in that dark place before Lance Armstrong was even born,' wrote Tina. 'In many ways it was even more devastating. In those days cancer was something you just didn't mention, a taboo word, a fearful prospect. All I could think was – he's only twenty-three and he has been handed his death warrant.'

'A training injury,' said the club physiotherapist of the crippling pain in his groin. 'It will wear off.' But it did not wear off, and twenty-four hours after waking up in agony, Bobby was on the operating table, having a testicle removed.

From the start to the end, Bobby and Tina Moore never mentioned the word *cancer*. It was an age where celebrities did not talk openly about fighting disease. No talk-show confessionals, no inspirational books, no mention of illness, or the raw courage it took to fight and beat it.

'Don't tell anyone what I'm in here for,' Bobby told his wife.

He did not know if he would live or die. He did not know if he would ever play football again. Tina said, 'What had happened struck at his livelihood, his masculinity, his very existence on the planet.' Returning from hospital, the young husband and wife held each other, watched *Top of the Pops*, and cried their eyes out.

Cancer kept Bobby Moore out of the game for just three months. Three months! These days footballers have longer out for twisting the cruciate ligaments in their poor little knees.

The following year, Moore captained West Ham when they beat TSV Munich 1860 in the European Cup Winners Cup Final at Wembley. And one year after that, he was holding aloft the World Cup.

His wife, who met him at the Ilford Palais when she was fifteen and he was sixteen, summed him up for all time with the three little words that went through her head as her twenty-five-year-old husband held aloft that World Cup. Only she – and his doctors and nurses – knew that in just eighteen months Bobby Moore had gone from a desperate fight against cancer to the eternal glory of that summer's day in 1966.

What a man, she thought. What a man.

For five years, all through the peak of his career, Bobby Moore had regular check-ups, and waited for the cancer to come back. Every ache and pain felt like the rumour of his premature death. But the public never knew about Moore's cancer until long after his death, when the disease – cancer of the colon this time – claimed him at the age of fifty-one. Yet there were clues.

When he was in remission, there were blue crosses on Moore's back, so the radiotherapist would miss his kidneys. Yet nobody ever said a thing.

Almost unbelievably, no journalist ever asked Bobby or Tina Moore about the real reason for those three months out of the game. In Bobby's lifetime, his greatest triumph of all, that successful battle against cancer as a twenty-three-year-old, would never be spoken of.

Already private and guarded, Bobby became even more isolated after the cancer. In that world of communal baths, he bathed alone. The word got around that he had lost a testicle in a training injury, but it was never really the subject of gossip or dressing-room levity. For there was something about Bobby Moore – a reserve, a poise, a seriousness – that did not encourage locker-room banter. And he was hard. With his blond hair, blue eyes and dimples, he had the face of a Botticelli angel, but the body of a bare-knuckle fighter. He may have looked like a film star, but Bobby Moore was made of East End concrete.

Even on that summer's day in 1966, Bobby Moore seems somehow apart from his teammates. Bobby Charlton is in tears. Nobby Stiles is cavorting. Many of them are overwhelmed with exhaustion and emotion. And yet even at that great shining moment, Bobby Moore is immaculate, composed, as though climbing this Everest was a walk in the park. There is no mistaking that broad, dimpled grin, and the pure joy of the moment, and yet, unlike the rest of the boys of '66, Bobby Moore does not seem overcome.

'He wasn't like us,' said Jackie Charlton. 'He was one of us, but he wasn't like us.'

That composure recalls the way he performed the classic Moore tackle – down on one knee, stealing the ball with the other foot, the perfection of his timing uncanny. Or the way he broke up an attack by chesting the ball down, then looking up and around and biding his time before finally releasing the ball – as he did to set Geoff Hurst off for that fourth and final goal in the 1966 World Cup Final.

From one end of the sixties to the other, Bobby Moore gave the impression that he was always in complete control.

Bobby Moore was from the other side of the sixties. The sixties of suits and ties, of always looking smart, always looking clean. Bobby liked the sharp, lean lines of the Mod look, and later Turnbull and Asser shirts, and big fat Windsor knots in his ties. But if you were from this side of the sixties, you would not be ready to grow your hair for another ten years. Bobby finally grew it in the seventies, but it never really worked with his tight blond curls. Born in 1941, the sixties coincided almost exactly with his twenties, and they were his time. Long hair didn't suit him. Neither did the seventies.

Bobby came from the side of the sixties that believed in gin and tonic, not LSD and bombers; early marriage and children, not groupies and sexual experimentation. Bobby Moore floated through the sixties on a river of alcohol, but it was hedonism from the old school. His was the sixties of enduring respect, of happily dipping your head to your monarch. When Bobby Moore climbed the steps of Wembley Stadium to receive the World Cup, he noticed that the Queen was wearing long, white gloves, and so he wiped his sweaty, muddy hands on the velvet lining of the royal box. In that moment of deference to his Queen, Moore looks like an English hero who has more in common with Wellington and Nelson than he does with any footballer of our own time.

But it was another age. The West Ham trio of Bobby Moore, Geoff Hurst and Martin Peters that won the World Cup all lived in suburban Essex, a few miles from each other, a few miles from Upton Park. Even when they were being shot for *Vogue*, Tina Moore thought of herself as a 'Gants Hill housewife'.

How impossibly down-home it all seems now. After winning the World Cup, the celebration dinner was at the Royal Garden Hotel in Kensington High Street. The wives were not invited, and the WAGS hadn't been invented. The wives – and most of those young men in their twenties were already married, already fathers – were fed in the Bulldog Chophouse in another part of the hotel. 'It was stag,' says Tina Moore.

She met her husband at midnight and they went to the Playboy Club on Park Lane. Burt Bacharach asked Victor Lownes, Hugh Hefner's right-hand man in London, to introduce him to the young England captain. Then young Mr and Mrs Moore went home to Gants Hill in Essex. Bobby Moore was restless the next day, couldn't settle to anything. Geoff Hurst, the hat-trick hero, mowed his lawn.

These were the early days of corporate sponsorship. Ford Motors gave the Moores an Escort, but it had a picture of a cartoon lion, World Cup Willie, the leering mascot of 1966, on the side, so they never went anywhere in it. And yet, for all the ordinariness of their home life, Bobby Moore became a global superstar on that summer's day in 1966, and for the rest of his days, although there would be disappointments and failure, he would always be fêted as a true hero.

'You don't often hear a man described as beautiful,' said Tina Moore in her book about her ex-husband. 'But that's what Bobby was – he looked like a young god who happened to play football. He was a complicated young god.'

The footballers of the Premiership make more in a year than Bobby Moore made in a lifetime. And yet it feels as though every one of them is living in his shadow. Who ever looked better in *Vogue* than Bobby Moore? Whoever came anywhere near what he achieved on that summer's day in 1966? Whoever looked more perfect for the role that history had chosen him for?

What was true of Elvis Presley is equally true of Bobby Moore. Before anyone did anything, Bobby Moore did everything.

The one lasting side effect of that first bout of cancer was an insomnia that stayed with him for the rest of his life. As swinging sixties England danced until dawn, or watched Ken Dodd and then went to bed, Bobby Moore slipped out of his striped pyjamas, got dressed, and wandered the streets of Essex all night.

After the World Cup, his life went from the back page to the front page. And yet there was a part of Bobby Moore that was always unreachable; his wife said that he hid 'behind a wall of politeness'. Bobby was rarely impressed by the celebrities he met, apart from his brief meeting with his idol Frank Sinatra. The photo of them together shows Bobby looking as star-struck as any young West Ham fan in the presence of their golden captain.

Like Sinatra, Moore was the only child of working-class parents. He lacked for everything, apart from all the things that matter, and grew up with a belief that he could do anything. Bobby Moore had a mother who ironed his football laces, and perhaps these torrents of unconditional love got him from the testicular cancer in 1964 to the World Cup in 1966.

In the Barking of his childhood they played their football in the streets – there were few cars – and it was here that Bobby honed his curiously erect, ramrod-straight style. Terry Venables, friend and neighbour, remembered, 'You had to learn to stay on your feet on concrete.'

Didier Drogba would have been fucked.

Bobby was always aspirational – he did not have the laughably fake posh accent of Sir Alf Ramsey (in reality another East End boy), and yet his was not quite a Cockney accent. Bobby was *well-spoken*, as they said in those East End–Essex borderlands. So was his wife. The child of an ambitious single mother, and the only girl in Dagenham with a pair of riding britches, Tina had had elocution lessons, and the young couple's hunger to better themselves chimed perfectly. The young Bobby Moore discovered and tore through smoked salmon, French cheese and Italian wine as though they were conquered countries. 'He always had lovely manners,' remembered Tina. 'It was in-built. But it became more polished. He watched people.'

He was obsessively professional. He could drink them all

under the table, even his hard-living mates George Best and Jimmy Greaves, but Bobby was fanatical about his fitness, and always ran off the extra calories the day after. He was pathologically tidy about the house, a cushion straightener, meticulous in his habits. He was fastidious – when he put on his trousers in a dressing room, he stood on the bench. When he went into a bar, he would count out twelve peanuts, and eat no more and no less. It is the kind of discipline that made him a world-beater.

Bobby was envied and loved even by the playboys, the bad lads, the other great ones. It wasn't the medals. It was the way Bobby Moore carried himself. George Best said, 'If I could wish for my son to turn out like someone, it would be Bobby Moore. He had no flaws. On the pitch he was immaculate. He was great with kids. It's a special quality. Knowing you're something special and yet not acting like you're something special.'

Bobby Moore's legend rests on 642 matches for West Ham, and three successful appearances at Wembley – the FA Cup Final of 1964, West Ham's victory in the European Cup Winners Cup Final in 1965, and then that summer's day in 1966. If the rest of his life was an anti-climax, then how could it be anything else?

He collected his MBE at Buckingham Palace, he had a part in Hollywood's attempt at football, *Hero*, he rode in a Rolls-Royce. Everyone wanted to shake his hand, everyone wanted to meet him. But there were money worries, and they never really went away.

In the 1975 FA Cup Final, Moore's new club Fulham lined up against West Ham United. At the end, when West Ham had run out easy winners, Bobby comforted his teammate Alan Mullery, who looks crushed by defeat. In contrast, Bobby seems relaxed, philosophical, even happy. It wasn't that he didn't care. But he did not look flattened, as he had when the West Germans knocked England out of the World Cup in Mexico in 1970. After the heights he had scaled, and the battles that he had fought, a loser's medal in his thirties must have seemed not like a tragedy but some small bonus.

And yet there were hundreds more senior matches to play at Craven Cottage, and decades of bad business deals, unhappy shots at small-time management and, a year before their silver wedding anniversary, divorce from Tina. Bobby – always a sex symbol but never a womaniser – fell in love with an airline stewardess called Stephanie Parlane. He married her just over a year before his death on 24th February 1993.

The football writer, Chris Lightbown, said of Bobby, 'His death made you feel as though you had lost contact with a better time. A more certain time. A time when good beat bad. A time when better values probably prevailed. A time that was more straightforward. A time that was cleaner. Because he had all of that. And he personified all of that. He cut across class in a way that not many people do in this country.'

Bobby Moore was the perfect England captain, because he embodied the best of England – dignity, restraint, and a quiet kind of courage. He had the strength that never needs to raise its voice. He was as hard as teak, and yet there was a genuine gentleness about him. His son and his daughter adored him. All children adored him.

At one point in the sixties, every woman in the land wanted to go to bed with him and yet for the best years of his life he remained a devoted family man. His wife once took off Michael Caine's glasses, just to confirm that – as she had suspected – Bobby was in fact much more handsome than the young movie star.

Bobby Moore was down to earth and yet he was a hero. At the dawn of our age of cut-price fame and increasingly disposable celebrity, Bobby was the real and unforgettable thing. He was loved, truly loved, by millions of people who had never met him. And we miss him still.

There are monuments to Bobby Moore. A statue at Upton Park. A tunnel named after him at Wembley Stadium, where men and boys relieve themselves in his honour. But the real monument to Bobby Moore is the love and affection and hope that he still inspires in the hearts of every English football fan.

And if that is his monument, then his epitaph is the thought that rang in the head of his twenty-four-year-old wife as she watched him hold up the World Cup on that lost summer's day.

What a man.

Eleven

The Gunfire
Next Door

There are men firing guns below my window.

The sound of gunfire is a cracking sound, a jagged, stretched-out sound that seems to split the air, to tear it apart, to rip it to shreds. *Crack*. It is the loudest noise I have ever heard in my life. Or perhaps it only seems that way. Nothing gets your attention quite like the sound of gunfire.

And I realise that this is a first for me. I have never heard guns fired in anger before, guns fired with the sole, cold-eyed intention of killing another human being.

The first time you hear gunfire is like losing your virginity, but without the sex.

I am at the window of my room in the Mandarin in Manila. My mate from Hong Kong is at the window with me. When the coup erupts we are, inappropriately enough, dressed for the gym. Another friend from Hong Kong is having a birthday party tomorrow, although it might get cancelled now that rebel soldiers have occupied the hotel next door, the Peninsula, and the army are trying to get them out. Our hotel has locked its doors, fearing an overspill of rebel troops. Nobody can get in or out. Tonight there will be a curfew and the streets of Manila will be empty by midnight. But this is better than a birthday party.

The rebels are stuck inside the Peninsula with what sounds like the entire army of the Philippines outside. *Crack-crack-crack* go the guns. It is a symphony of gunfire – single shots, emphatic and murderous, mixed with stuttering streams of automatic fire, *Crackcrackcrackcrackcrack*. For the men on the receiving end of all that gunfire it must sound like the end of the world.

The rebels have made a tactical mistake. They have evacuated all the guests from the Peninsula and so the army are going in without restraint. There are suitcases and bags abandoned everywhere and all the innocent bystanders are hotfooting it through the business district of Makati. *Crack. Crack. Crackcrackcrackcrackcrack.*

You can't really tell what's happening. The events below my window are suddenly the lead story on BBC World and CNN, but even with all that live rolling news it is hard to say what is going on.

We can see from the TV that the rebels have barricaded the glass doors of the Peninsula and the army are trying to drive an armoured car through them. Then there is a sudden eruption of gunfire and a lone soldier at a makeshift roadblock below my window throws himself face down on the road. My friend's grin grows wider.

The gunfire feels like it is in the atmosphere, as undeniable as the weather, and it takes an effort not to flinch every time it tears the air apart. I am sort of peeping out of the window but my mate is standing upright, the macho fool, as if daring a stray round to do for him. *Crackcrackcrackcrackcrack.* The sound is deafening, or at least that's how it seems. Are the guns really so loud or do they just seem loud? No, they really are that loud. There is no ignoring the sound of guns.

And I realise something else about that sound.

I love it.

My father always thought me a lesser man than he because I had never heard that sound. And he was right. I have no doubt at all that he was right.

That is the price we pay for being children of peace, for being cosseted little princes who got to worry about career trajectories and recreational drugs and our relationship issues. We are forever lesser men than the men who have heard the guns because we have not been tested.

Not that today gives me the right to compare myself to my father. But the gunfire is real enough and close enough, and I half suspect that my mate's head will explode at any moment from some rogue burst of automatic fire.

I think of my dad all the time today, and I know that you could make a million pounds and fly a million miles and bed a million girls but if you have not heard the guns fired in anger, then you have not really lived, not as he lived.

The exhilaration of today – the mad fun of the gunfire – is mingled with disappointment, for I know that I have still never been tested in the way that my father and his entire generation were tested, and I never will be.

The soldiers outside my window are not trying to kill me and my mate. They would no doubt hate it – and get into a lot of trouble – if one of us was shot. Even in the middle of a coup, we are protected, fretted over, the pampered, grown-up little princes of peace.

That is just the way the historic dice fell. My old man fought at Monte Cassino. I had Morrissey come round for tea. My dad had black fragments of German shrapnel in his body until the day he died, and the only competition I can muster is that I probably have a stray chunk of amphetamine sulphate up my nose from sharing my stash with Johnny Rotten on Jubilee Day.

I think of my old man today and I know, with all my heart, that I am the lucky one.

So why do I envy him?

I will tell you what the guns do not sound like. They do not sound like any twelve-bore shotgun fired at fur or feather. They do not sound like the air rifles of your childhood fields, or the popguns you get at fairgrounds. These guns have the sound of murder in them.

But it is not a war. (Would we prefer a war?) Although for the next few hours this coup attempt will be the biggest story in the world, what's happening beyond my window is more like something from a Graham Greene novel – a little local conflict, more farce than tragedy.

Why have the rebels occupied a five-star hotel? Why didn't they commandeer a TV station or an army barracks? And why didn't the army – who have now successfully driven their armoured car through the plate-glass windows of the Peninsula – put on their gas masks *before* they sprayed the hotel with tear gas? The army boys look a bit silly, running back out of the hotel, gagging and coughing and eyes burning, to put on their masks after unloading their tear gas. Still, there is one thing you can't deny.

This is fun.

But guns sicken me. Don't they?

Of course they do.

Guns are a growth industry in Britain, flooding in from the former Communist hellholes of the world, and my spirits sink when I read about another mindless shooting, another teenager dead, when I hear that my old neighbourhood is torn apart by the hip-hop fantasies of cruel, simple-minded children and their loathsome weapons. But this is different. This is the Philippines. This is tropical gunfire, this is the sound of shots being fired under the palm trees, of automatic weapons being unloaded as the sun goes down over Manila Bay and the lights come on all over Makati.

And in a situation like this, there is no denying the romance of guns, the glamour of guns. You can see the attraction. Nothing gets the world's attention quite like a gun being fired. It is about power that can't be denied. Perhaps this is what those stupid children feel when they are killing each other and the blameless innocents on the mean streets of London and Manchester and Liverpool.

We are not like soldiers, my mate and I, as we stand by the window and listen to the *crackcrackcrack* of the coup being suppressed. We are both the sons of Royal Marines, but as we stand at that window we are more like war correspondents than soldiers. We are like the narcissistic loons who flew to Vietnam and Cambodia just before the white man fled old Indo-China forever. Like the war correspondent who is free to risk his hide or catch a cab to the airport, there is a major element of slumming in our perusal of the coup. We are just here for the *crackcrackcrack*, for the guns fired in anger.

My mate points out how stupid that expression is – *guns fired in anger*. When you have been in the presence of gunfire, and heard the guns in all their deafening terror and violence and fury, you understand that they can be fired no other way. Guns are always fired in anger.

You can taste the fear: in the men firing the weapons – all those skinny teenage soldiers huddled under the Peninsula's five-star flower arrangements, pointing their guns up at the higher floors – and in the men they are shooting at.

Gunfire gives you that feeling you get when you are coming home from a funeral, when you are pulling off the black tie and wiping the grave dirt from your shoes. You are glad to be alive.

And with every *crackcrackcrack* I know what a fleeting ride this life is, and how you only get to go round once, and how much I am looking forward to the first San Miguel of the night, and hearing them play 'Lust for Life' in Wild West and 'Another Girl, Another Planet' in Flamingo and 'Shake That' in Jools, and watching the neon lights shimmer in the Third World darkness. *Crackcrackcrack.* It's just like Paulie Walnuts said at the end of *The Sopranos*:

'In the midst of death we are in life – or is it the other way round?'

On my first day at work, I heard a bomb go off. I was in Cheapside when the IRA detonated their Old Bailey bomb, and it sounded like a door in heaven slamming shut. *Whooosh.* All the air sucked out of the atmosphere, with a dreadful and murderous finality. It was a sickening sound, but it did not make me think of my father, and how I was a bit more like him – and more worthy to be his son – now that I had heard a bomb explode. The bomb was scary, horrific, sickening. The gunfire is different. Why is it different? Because it sounds like what we have been missing. It sounds like what has been lacking in our fortunate lives.

I know how stupid that seems. My friend and I both have young families relying on us, and we want to watch our children grow up, and why risk your life in a botched coup that has nothing to do with you? But there is no denying the heightened quality to the day when, to paraphrase Julie Andrews, the hills are alive with the sound of gunfire.

Then all at once the coup has collapsed. Rebels are giving interviews on CNN and BBC World. They are quite emotional, but they have also been tear-gassed, so everybody's eyes are streaming with both real feeling and toxic chemicals. Then soldiers haul the rebels off to a waiting troop carrier to take them into custody. But this being the Philippines, the doors of the vehicle are locked and everyone stands around wondering what to do next. The guns are silent.

'Definitely the high point of the trip,' says my friend, and we go to the gym.

My father would have laughed himself dizzy. My old man would have heard my theories about how modern man lacks danger, and challenge, and an awareness of the fragility of life, and he would have split his sides. A coup is not a war. Guns are not frightening until they are pointing at you. And an afternoon watching a coup as if it was a sporting event is not the same as watching your friends die, and knowing with total certainty that you are not fighting for freedom or democracy but for the men by your side.

My father would have been right to laugh, but his laughter would have missed something and that is our craving to feel like real men for once in our soft little lives.

And they were real guns, Dad. You can't take that away from me.

Twelve

Performance Anxiety

Men – do you suffer from PA?

You don't know PA? Oh, but you do, you do – you know it in your bones, in your blood, in your wayward wood. Or should that be your fear of the wayward wood?

PA gives men more sleepless nights than ME, VAT and the EU put together. And it is always there. Women only have to suffer PMT once a month. But for many men, PA is a constant thorn in the side – and in the darkest regions of the pants.

PA – performance anxiety – is not the same as sexual dysfunction. PA is not in your bed – it's all in your head. Premature ejaculation, losing an erection, coming in your Calvins – these things can happen to any man. Okay, so it's not much fun if they all happen on the same date, but they can happen.

But PA is not an unfortunate one-off. Performance anxiety is in the toxic air we inhale. It is the reason why so many young men are doing something that would have been unthinkable even in the dying days of the last century.

They are reaching for Viagra.

These men are in their thirties, their twenties and their teens.

Incredible but true. Now why would a teenage male animal want to take those little blue pills? At an age when he can get an erection just by looking at the legs on a Habitat table, why would a teenage boy want or need artificial stimulation? Because, like so many of his brothers, he suffers from chronic performance anxiety.

Dr John Dean, a specialist in sexual medication, says that as recently as ten years ago it would have been very rare for a man in his thirties to use Viagra. Today, says Dr Dean, the thirty-something on Viagra has become commonplace.

And Dr John Tomlinson, trustee of the Sexual Dysfunction Association, reports that he is hearing from an 'enormous' number of men between the ages of eighteen and forty who are worried about sexual problems. 'Men may feel emasculated by modern women, and feminism has taken its toll,' says Dr Tomlinson.

Performance anxiety is a physiological, psychological and emotional fact. And it is reaching epidemic proportions. For many men, having sex is no longer enough. Even having good sex is no longer enough. You have to pound away with the stamina of a porn star until she is begging for more, and then begging you to stop. Men fantasise so much about all this porn-star pounding, that a bit of everyday pounding in the real world is becoming increasingly difficult for them.

An acquaintance confided that he was so intent on giving both his wife and his mistress high-grade orgasms that for him the sex had been siphoned of all pleasure. His sex life had

deteriorated into a stressful chore because of all this damn
performance anxiety. His wedding tackle had become a cross
to bear. His meat and two veg were now a ball and chain.

This man was getting more sex than he could handle in the
kind of set-up that he had always craved – a beautiful young
wife waiting at home, and a compliant lover whom he could
see when the mood was upon him. But he was not having
quality sex. He was having junk sex.

And none of it was fun. Not with the bride, nor the bit on
the side. Because PA had drained it all of delight, or even the
possibility of delight. Sex turned into a chore, a duty, like taking
out the recycling bins, and then it became something far worse:
a test that he could only fail. An examination where his manhood
could only be found wanting. Not often enough, not big enough,
not hard enough and not for long enough. What's a guy to
do? He woke up one morning with a bad case of those old
performance anxiety limp-dick blues.

And this is a man talking about his wife and mistress –
women who know him well, and who would presumably be
willing to cut him some slack in the sack. But every time he
made love, it had to be a Barry White twelve-inch. Classic PA.
If that's what it's like for a husband and lover, can you imagine
the performance anxiety pressing down on a twenty-something
man leading some modern miss to his futon for the first time?
Perhaps you can imagine it all too easily.

My suspicion is that PA used to be confined to young single
men who had watched too much porn who were going out

with young single women who had seen too many re-runs of *Sex and the City*. But now PA is spreading to the guy in the long-term relationship, and to the married man. That's the terrible thing about PA. No man is truly immune. On all our report cards, it says – *Must do better. See me.*

Traditionally, men in long-term relationships didn't get PA because when you are with a woman who knows you that well – in the is-it-good-for-you-baby? Biblical sense – then she knows that sometimes you can go all night long, and at other times you might go on from midnight to about five past. But all that is changing.

PA is so prevalent now that no heterosexual man is safe. Do gay men also suffer from PA? Perhaps not. But for the straight guy, it's a PA world out there. You can see it in your spam.

For every junk email I get from kindly Nigerian bankers requesting the details of my bank account so they can send me some free money from Lagos, I must get ten promising to take me down from the crucifix of my performance anxiety.

Stronger-longer-harder, they promise. *Thicker-thicker. Add extra inches. Viagra. Cialis. Tramadol. Hairy Goat Weed Virility Patch. Drive her crazy.*

But in a world where healthy men in their twenties and thirties are taking an anti-impotence drug designed for geezers in their sixties and seventies who have had prostate surgery, we are driving nobody crazy but ourselves.

There is no reason why young men should be taking a pill prescribed to relieve impotence – apart from performance anxiety, which they would see as the best reason of all. But this stuff wasn't actually designed to make your hot date go with a bang or five.

There is the famous story of a Hollywood actor – a mainstream arthouse sort of star – who was going on a first date with one of the great sex symbols of our time. And he was nervous. Who wouldn't be? He had bedded starlets, co-stars and smalltown beauty queens galore, and yet he was worried that he might get into bed with this woman – this fantasy figure for millions – and disappoint her. He had performance anxiety and he had it bad. So what did he do? He reached for the blue pills. And he ended up with an erection that lasted for forty-eight hours. He describes it as one of the most unpleasant experiences of his life. Inevitably, the sex symbol got away. He lost her because of PA.

If he had trusted his body – in all its humanity and fallibility and unpredictability – then who knows what might have happened? It may have been all he dreamed of. But he wanted it to be perfect, he wanted it to be better than perfect. He wanted her to have orgasms that would rattle her Golden Globes. He gave it all away for the sake of PA. Because the drugs didn't work. Apart from the perma-boner – which he would probably been quite pleased about if he was seventy years old and in remission from prostate cancer – they gave him the kind of headache that meant he could not even think straight, let alone love straight. But apart from the fact that he was out on the town with a sex symbol, there is nothing remotely unusual about that actor. He is merely a product of our fretful PA age.

There are now a generation of young men out there who have imbibed performance anxiety as if it was their mother's milk. At an age when they should be racking up the sexual memories that will last them a lifetime, they are fretting that they might not be able to cut the Colman's when the lights go down. That PA mindset does not lead to sexual ecstasy – or even sexual impotence. It leads to celibacy. In the end you become like the man who had a wife and mistress and lay awake at night worrying that he might not be giving total satisfaction. You conclude – why bother?

Your grandfather didn't worry about his performance. Granddad thought that sex was something that men enjoyed and women endured. Nobody wants to revive Granddad's selfish ways. For the last fifty years, men have been made aware that sexual pleasure is not stag, and that's a fine thing. But the bad old days of sexual selfishness have not been eradicated, they have merely been inverted. If the old boys worried far too little about their partner's satisfaction then the new men worry far too much.

Demanding women are often asked to carry the can for male PA, but men have largely brought it on themselves with their own unrealistic expectations. The explosion of home-entertainment pornography that arrived with broadband has done young men no good at all. The sexual image that we now have of our gender is largely based on men who fuck for a living. Which is as silly as going over the park for a kick-about and expecting to play like Ronaldo.

Even porn stars are mere flesh, blood and wayward wood. Doesn't every porn set include the fluffer, whose job it is to keep the leading man pointing due north? Biologically, men are less capable of duplicity than women. They can always fake an orgasm. But we can never fake an erection.

PA is born from fantasy images of men – and of women too. And it is not restricted to adult websites. Why do we persist in believing that the insatiable sirens of *Sex and the City* are real? Knowing that one of the actresses is actually a middle-aged lesbian who has a girlfriend who looks like Johnny Vegas doesn't make any difference. We – and our women – suck up images of women who can't get enough of that funky stuff and import the fiction into the real world. Where it becomes, if not exactly true, then something to aspire to after a bucket of Bacardi Breezers.

Sexual liberation was meant to set us free. Brave men shagged in the mud of Woodstock so that we might have healthy sex lives. But the free and easy swinging has stopped. The care-free grinding has ground to a halt. PA is turning men into nervous wrecks.

We now have a peculiarly old-fashioned view of sex, where one participant is *not allowed* to merely gorge themselves on pleasure.

Once it was the woman, and now it is the man.

Like that poor chap who is so concerned about the orgasms

of his wife and mistress that he forgets all about his own, men are being struck down by sexual self-consciousness.

Get over it. Don't think about it so much. Male sexual technique has improved beyond all recognition in recent generations. These days some of us can even locate a clitoris without a compass.

Yet every man is past his sexual peak before he even knows how to talk to girls. When I was seventeen, I bought a packet of condoms and was reusing them before the night was out. The sap wasn't just rising, it was volcanic. Flights were being cancelled. But Mother Nature is finished with you by the time you are out of your teens. Which doesn't mean that you are ever finished with her.

If you are not recovering from cancer, then you are never so over the hill that you need a pill. Young men taking Viagra is as obscene as children worrying about their weight.

Men are becoming pill-popping male eunuchs endlessly obsessed with dishing out orgasms. Put down that Viagra. Throw away the hairy goat weed virility patch. Hold the L-Arginine. Ditch the junk sex. Performance anxiety? Relax. Don't do it.

It is a wonderful thing to give a woman pleasure. But step out from the shadow of your spam, and maybe save some for yourself.

Thirteen

Love Handles, Actually

Jeremy Clarkson approached me on the beach. We stood there in our swimming trunks, the Caribbean wind whipping up the legs of our Speedos. Grown men. Half-naked. Never met before. Those of a nervous disposition – look away now.

I had seen him in the lounge at Gatwick. And I did not want to be unfriendly, but at the same time I didn't want to be like some brainless *Top Gear* fan talking about the new camshaft on the Turbo 911. Surely he has enough of all that? So I let him be. I thought I might say hello on the plane. But his seat was a bit further back than mine.

'Jeremy,' I now said, as we stood there, our nipples stirring under the toasty Bajan sun. I felt like I should explain my initial coolness. 'I didn't want to be the guy who came up to you and started talking about the new Ford Mondeo.'

But Clarkson wasn't listening. He didn't care. His eyes scanned the golden sands of Barbados and settled on a local sleeping under a palm tree.

'Pretending to sleep,' Clarkson said. 'Just pretending. Paparazzi.' He shot me a look. 'So if you go in the water – suck your gut in.'

I looked at Jeremy and I looked at the sleeping man. And I looked at Clarkson's body and I looked at my own.

And I thought – Wait a minute.

If paparazzi took a picture of me frolicking in the crystal waters of the Caribbean, and that picture appeared in a mass-circulation publication, then what would happen? Would a picture of me in my swimming trunks provoke derision and wide-spread mockery and contempt from my peers? Or would it result in soaring book sales, increased sexual opportunities, and undiluted adoration from a grateful female population?

I would have put my last Bajan dollar on the latter. Because every week I spend many hours in the gym – punching and crunching, sweating and groaning, being cajoled, urged on and screamed at. I spend far longer in the gym than I ever do in restaurants, pubs or bars. Or galleries, cinemas and theatres.

After work and my family, the gym is what I do. What I am.

My body is a temple. Okay, so perhaps after all these years it is not quite the Taj Mahal. But it is at least a charming provincial church.

Or maybe I am kidding myself.

Jeremy Clarkson was clearly trying to be nice. He was trying to do me a favour. And I appreciate that. But he saw me as the same as him. A man – no longer in the first flush of youth

– who could be made a public mockery, a total laughing stock, by innocently having a paddle on his holiday.

Clarkson is not fat. In many ways, he is the opposite of fat. He is big. He is long. But he has the belly of a man who spends a long time behind steering wheels. He has a driver's body. And a smoker's body. Whereas I have the body of someone who walks everywhere and worries about his weight as much as a member of Girls Aloud. I have a body that is fit for purpose. At least, I thought I did.

'Suck it in,' Clarkson advised as he turned away, and the paparazzi stirred under his palm tree.

They say that Pilates lengthens, strengthens and tones – my penis is thinking about taking it up.

Because you have to do something, don't you? If you do nothing – then what happens? You put on a kilo a year – oh, it is the easiest thing in the world – and you do that for five years, ten years, twenty – and before you know it, the fresh-faced, lean-limbed boy has transformed into a shagged-out old loser man, and the good life is over forever, and the best will always be behind you. Because nothing – nothing! – signifies your status in this world more than your fitness – or your lack of fitness.

The tyranny of fitness – it simply wasn't like this in the past.

This obsession with the firmness of our abdominal muscles, the fascination with our muscle tone, the need to get on the scales and let them pass cruel judgement – in the past it was, frankly, always a chick thing.

I remember the commercials of my childhood. 'If you can pinch more than an inch – you may be overweight!' 'Chocolates? Maltesas!'

Was this fear of excess fat aimed at my father? My brown ale-drinking, Full English-scoffing father? No – those ads were aimed at my mother. My slim, eternally whippet-thin mother. Mum was the one who was required to fret about the fat. Her and all the women in the developed world. Men did not care about this stuff. Men were above obsessing about their physical appearance.

Not any more.

Our concept of success – financial, professional, emotional, social, sexual and spiritual success – is bound up completely with what in the end is skin-deep. Our physical appearance. Our fitness level. A man's firmness – that's what matters most. Not the size of his wallet, or his heart, or his member, or even his brain. The size of his biceps.

But now a terrible knowledge haunts men, too. Isn't that why our lives revolve around this pathological obsession with health, with fitness, with the definition of our abs? Isn't that why we spend longer in gyms than we do in church?

Because, unlike our fathers and our grandfathers, we now know that it applies to us too.

We all lose our charms in the end.

*   *   *

What a strange, turbulent relationship men have with their bodies.

For years – all through our teens, and the first half of our twenties – our bodies are adoring partners, blithely taken for granted, a childhood sweetheart, casually neglected – with drink, with drugs, with inappropriate food consumed in the wee small hours.

That arrogance, those easy assumptions, that horrible behaviour – treating your body like someone who will always love you, no matter how badly you behave – soon passes. One day soon after your twenty-fifth birthday, you look in the mirror and it is there before you. The invoice for the folly of youth. The bill for every line of cocaine and drunken kebab. This account is much overdue, the mirror says. Please remit.

You can't miss it. There's a certain blurring of the hairline. Or perhaps a sagging of the chin. And – always – the smudging of the features that a few extra pounds can bring. Now you know, and now you will never forget.

To make this relationship work, it will take a lot of effort. But you are always fighting a losing battle. Or rather, as you do your best to look good on the long, slow slide to the grave, it is a war that you can never really win. That's the thing that anyone who cares about their fitness learns. It never ends.

You can do your abdominal crunches until the mad cows come home. You can lift your weights. You can do your martial art or your boxing. Run that marathon or pound that treadmill – run until your body feels as though it has been in a blender.

You look good for your age, you think. You look good for any age. You are firmer, and lighter, and tighter than younger men. But you can never stop. Run, fit boy, run.

You nosh your Viper bars so you can train harder for longer. You religiously drink your Recovermax – the ultimate research-proven, post-training recovery drink. You bookmark the website for Maximuscle. And you do it until you can look at yourself naked in the mirror and feel, well, I guess it is a sort of pervy pride.

You think – not bad, boy. Not bad at all.

And then Jeremy Clarkson comes up to you on the beach and advises you to suck your gut in.

Successful fat people have gone the way of the dinosaur, the dodo and Simon Dee. Once upon a time, successful fat people were among us. But they walk the Earth no more. They simply do not exist. You do not even see successful, attractive people who are slightly out of shape.

Those stolen pictures on the beach, gloated over by the tabloids – why do they mean so much? Why is it so reassuring to see the cellulite on the upper thighs of a sex symbol, or the potbelly drooping over the trunks of a cocky TV presenter?

Because a lean hard body means a happy life.

And a soft, flabby carcass means failure, melancholy and dashed expectations.

Fair enough, really. It takes effort to stay in shape. It takes discipline, and denial, and determination. Anyone can fall to pieces. Like body, like life. If you can't take control over your waist-line, then why should you expect to take charge of your career, your love life, your social sphere?

When I was a lad, being fit was corny. You gave yourself to sport when you were little, and then you grew up and gave yourself to sex and drugs and rock and roll.

There was something unseemly – something suburban, some-thing very straight and square – about grown men who cared about their fitness. Did Johnny Rotten do press-ups? Did Johnny Marr work on the free weights?

Only Mick Jagger was what once was called a fitness fanatic – in the years before we were all fitness fanatics. It is no co-incidence that it is Jagger who ends the game as the winner – the one who has known more beautiful women, and made more money, and owned more homes, and burned his image into our mass consciousness. Of course – because Jagger always went running. Naturally he was the one who got Carla Bruni.

Why did I ever believe that physical fitness was a childish toy? But that is exactly what it was – school sports day, jumpers for goalposts, perhaps a bit of weekend football until you found a girl who liked you. I thought I could put sport and fitness aside, treat it all like the egg-and-spoon race. Once, being fit was about how you were young. Now, being fit is about how we get older.

We can't take anyone seriously unless they take their fitness seriously. Politicians are now obliged to be semi-Olympians. You would never have got, say, Harold Wilson or Lady Thatcher putting on the Asics Gel Nimbus for a run round the park with the security team. But since Blair and his kickabouts with Kevin Keegan, all of them have serious fitness on their CV.

If you are a party leader, it is not enough to work out. You have to be seen to work out. William Hague can bang his head against the judo mat in the privacy of his own *dojo*, but David Cameron has to be seen in full flight. So did Gordon Brown, even if running came as naturally to him as levitating. Politicians run the way they once kissed babies. It is meant to be a sign that they are worthy to lead us.

Throwing yourself into fitness can backfire – when Jimmy Carter's legs went to jelly on a jog, and he was seen gulping for air like a drowning man, history was destined to portray him as a minor, one-term president, a peanut farmer who was promoted beyond his ability. Carter got caught out learning what we all soon discover. You can't look cool when you are pushing yourself to the limit.

But it is not just image. Keeping fit brings down blood pressure, lowers cholesterol, reduces weight, extends your life and makes sexual activity seem a good idea. It puts some calm into lives full of stress.

We don't endure all this pain because we want to be fit. We endure all this pain because we want to be sane.

I watch Clarkson walk away and enter the beach bar of the Coral Reef. From the back, he doesn't look as though he is carrying that Ferrari paunch.

But it's the gut where it always shows. It's the old love handles that you have to beat into submission. Tame those abdominal muscles, and you can conquer the universe.

I watch Clarkson go. From behind Jeremy looks like a big guy, a bit skinny even. From behind he has nothing to fear from that paparazzi under the palm tree.

He should try working out.

Fourteen

Man and Boy Racer

There were always cars.

Before girls, before drugs – before everything, apart from music and football – there were cars.

A passport to freedom. A ticket to adventure. A penis substitute before you had even realised that you had a penis.

If you grew up somewhere between the city and the country, then cars were what you lived for. And quite frequently, cars were what killed you.

For we drove years before we were legally allowed to do so. We drove cars without a licence, insurance or parental permission. We drove cars without due care. We drove too fast, we drove drunk, we drove without seatbelts. Indeed, when I was an Essex teenager in the seventies, wearing a seatbelt would have been like wearing a flowery dress. It did not happen.

You needed luck to survive that kind of car culture. And sometimes, the luck would run out. No one I knew was shot or stabbed or kicked to death. None of my mates died of natural causes. But there were wrecks by the side of those wild roads that had claimed schoolmates, and friends, and the brothers of friends. Sometimes a bunch of roaring boys would go for a ride and never come back. We were car crazy back then.

And I wonder where it went – this passion, this abiding obsession, this true love of cars. Now I look at the cars in my driveway – a BMW X5, a Mini Cooper – and it is exactly like looking into the eyes of someone you loved in the long, long ago.

When you think – But what did I ever see in them?

Those shiny new cars on my driveway mean nothing to me. They are not my multiple indefinite-entry visa to a better world of thrills and spills, speed and danger, fun and fulfilment. They mean no more to me than any other household appliance. It is a strangely depressing thought.

Because when I was eleven years old my friends and I bought a Morris Minor for £10 from some colourful travelling folk and all summer long we drove that pre-historic banger around a bumpy, sloping field. I had never known such pure, undiluted ecstasy before – and I wonder how many times I have experienced it since.

Just a bunch of pre-teen boys in a Morris Minor that cost ten quid – and yet we knew the kind of car-related joy that Brian Wilson, Chuck Berry and Bruce Springsteen wrote songs about.

That was where I lost my car virginity, in an Essex field with that Morris Minor. And it was so good that it should have been the start of a love affair that lasted a lifetime. I should be watching *Top Gear* every week. I should be getting excited when Jeremy, James and Richard start salivating about the new Testarossa.

But these days cars don't get me hard. They just bore me stiff.

Twentieth-century boys learned to drive the way previous generations learned to hunt, or fish, or paint their private parts with woad.

Driving was as inevitable as kicking a ball around or taking your .22 air rifle over the fields to shoot at birds — and each other. For years — summer after summer after summer — we dreamed of being old enough to take our driving test.

I took my first test on my seventeenth birthday, arriving dressed like Steve McQueen in *Le Mans*. The poster copy for *Le Mans* remains tattooed on my heart — 'Let Steve McQueen take you for a ride in the country. The country is France. The ride is one hundred and fifty miles per hour.'

Yeah, baby! Harrington jacket. White roll-neck. Black leatherette racing gloves. Ray-Bans. Plus of course, my L-plates.

I failed.

Terribly, hopelessly. There not being much call for the old mirror-signal-manoeuvre routine when piloting a Morris Minor around a field, where the only thing you might hit was the farmer's wife or the odd rabbit.

Did failing my test matter? It mattered more than anything in the world. I wept all the way home. I choked on my inconsolable grief, at my failure – as a mannish boy, as a car nut, as a Steve McQueen acolyte. Hot bitter tears stained the front of my Harrington jacket, and those loathsome L-plates.

But then I took it again, dressed in glasses and a suit and tie, like some kind of librarian.

And I fooled the bastards.

And I passed.

And then there was no stopping me.

I can understand why someone might love cars.

It is not an incomprehensible passion to me – not the way that a love of cricket or jazz or anal sex is incomprehensible – because I have loved cars too. I have been breathless with excitement as I slipped behind the wheel. Not for some aesthetic reason – and not because I admired the engine, or I could see they had really improved the camshaft, or any of that.

But because cars meant freedom.

I came back from that second, successful test and asked my dad if I could drive his car around the block. He reluctantly said okay, but told me that my mum was putting the kettle on so I should be right back. I promised. And took off in his big company car boat – a Vauxhall Fiasco or something of the sort. I picked up my girlfriend. And we were gone for eighteen hours.

Just driving. I knew that when I finally went home my old man would be apoplectic with rage. But it did not matter a damn. Because I was driving.

And those were the days when simply driving was enough.

Before I passed my test I would often spend weekends with a friend whose parents were divorced. He lived with his dad, who would usually be off on some romantic adventure on a Saturday night. So my friend would grab a set of his father's car keys – his dad had a fine selection of wheels – and we would go for a midnight drive.

Under-age, unlicensed, uninsured – some cider may have been consumed – and in love. In love with cars, in love with life. The two were inseparable.

Once we were filling the tank at a petrol station when a cop car pulled in. In a panic, my friend quickly drove off – with the petrol pump still attached to the car. But the cops didn't notice!

It was like being Bonnie and Clyde. That was what cars could do – they could make a couple of suburban idiots like us, living in the back of beyond, feel as though we were . . . truly alive.

Only cars could do this for you.

Only cars could set you free.

*   *   *

You got the car because without the car you would never get the girl.

This is what it was like – in Billericay and in New Jersey and in Modesto, California, and everywhere in between. In the developed world of the late twentieth century, you began your life as a consumer, and as a sexual entity, by getting a car.

Your car promised everything. It meant sex. It meant status. It meant liberation. Getting your first car was like getting out of the jail you had grown up in. The moment the keys jangled in the pocket of your 501s, suddenly you could see all the stars in the heavens.

My first car was a green and cream Ford Anglia. A snip at £95. It was all right once it got going, but could prove highly strung when woken from its slumber. Turning on the ignition – well, you never truly knew how that was going to work out. Sometimes it just couldn't be bothered.

One afternoon I met my girlfriend outside her sixth-form college. She came out with her laughing friends as I lounged on my Ford Anglia like car-crazy John Milner in *American Graffiti*, like Steve McQueen in *Le Mans*, like James Dean in my dreams.

Watched by her envious pals at the bus stop, my girlfriend slipped into the passenger seat of the Ford Anglia, tugging modestly at the hem of her hot pants. But my car wouldn't start.

It really, really would not start.

The bus came.

The friends left.

And eventually my girlfriend left too. With my best mate, as I recall.

But I kept the car.

Now, driving is a chore. Driving is a bore. As a transcendent experience, it is like my old Ford Anglia. It doesn't get started. Where did the love go?

There is something pornographic about car culture because it is entirely based on fantasy. Men dream about cars they will never own the way they fantasise about women they will never know. The hot wheels that will bring out your inner Jenson Button are as much of a wet dream as the hot woman who goes wild at a glimpse of your rather ordinary meat and two veg.

Nothing wrong with a bit of the old make-believe. But those open roads in the commercials don't exist in the real world. As I look down from the cockpit of my BMW X5, all I see is stagnant traffic, and roadworks, and speed cameras.

All these cars that could have given Steve McQueen a run for his money – what's the point exactly? You can only do 70 mph in this country. And when someone does much, much more, and gets done for speeding, or for killing a child, then they don't seem very much like Steve McQueen. They just seem pathetic.

And yet this I cannot deny – driving was once like kissing the face of God.

*   *   *

Before I could vote, I traded in the Ford Anglia for a brand-new Ford Escort.

That Escort, newly born in a manger in holy Dagenham, smelled like liberation. A perfume of leather, paint, metal, oil and rubber, a scent to make you lose your mind, and your marbles.

I could not even remotely afford that car. I got it on tick. I emptied my pockets and sold my soul to the devil. I would work for years in menial jobs to own that car.

And yet it was a bargain.

I loved my brand-new Escort – truly loved it. But somewhere between then and now, that part of my heart has died – or perhaps reserved itself for other things.

It's not about getting older. The whole *Top Gear* masturbatory fantasy world is kept alive by men on the wrong side of thirty, forty, fifty even. They never lose that passion. It probably increases with age.

I have a close friend with multiple Porsche 911s – and I can see the attraction. A Porsche 911 is more than a beautiful piece of engineering – it is a barrier against mortality, and somehow gives you a firm grip on all the things that are always being lost. Our youth, our future, our fun. I have spent a lot of time tooling around in his Porsche 911s and they have been some of the happiest times of my life.

But being in a Porsche 911 when you don't really and truly love cars is like being in church when you don't believe in God. When you have lost your faith, then you can't fake it – no matter how much you feel you may be missing.

I want to believe. I know my life would be infinitely richer if I could believe – in God, in Porsche. But it is just not in me any more. I had my faith and lost it.

I am a car heretic. Now my BMW sits in the atrophied traffic and I wonder how I ever believed that cars would set me free. These days they seem to imprison me. Yet without the driving years, and all the summers when I was the boy in a Brian Wilson song, I know that my life would have been greatly diminished.

In the end, it wasn't about sex. Cars – when they wouldn't start, when they gave up the ghost on the way home, when I had to get out and push – probably lost me many more girls than they ever won me.

But without the cars, without the nights spent bombing around those Essex highways like a cider-crazed hillbilly, something would have stayed out of reach.

You got a car. That is what boys did. And even when you got out and watched it quietly expire by the side of the A127, and the girl caught a cab, those wheels were the sweetest thing in your life.

Because even when your car would not start, you knew your life had begun.

Fifteen

Junk Sex

Ah, but it is a degraded, despoiled age we are living in, where everything seems a corrupt imitation of what it used to be, an age where the letter has been replaced by junk mail, and the Sunday roast has made way for junk food, and where a blissful, restorative eight hours' kip has become junk sleep, where you toss and turn, and wake too soon, and rise from your bed exhausted.

Junk nation. Junk planet. Junk age.

And worst of the lot is junk sex – sex when you really wished you had saved that erection for later, sex when you pumped it up when you didn't really need it, sex that you remember with the same indifference as last night's takeaway curry.

Don't pretend you don't know what I'm talking about – junk sex has the quality of having your teeth professionally cleaned, or filling in your VAT return. No, it's worse than that – because junk sex is not something that you really, really have to do every three months. Indeed, a man having junk sex is frequently a man who is struggling to maintain interest.

Junk sex is like the bell going on *Mastermind*. I've started so I'll finish.

Why is there an epidemic of junk sex? Why has sex gone the way of food, mail and sleep? Because there is just too much of it around. Twenty-first-century sex is like television – there is more of it than there ever was, but that doesn't mean that the overall quality has gone up. Junk sex is not like real sex at all. It's not even like watching TV. Junk sex is more like channel surfing. You can't deny that you are doing it, but you don't know why.

What once kept heterosexual young men in line, and prevented an outbreak of junk sex, was the mores of heterosexual young women. They just didn't want it as much – as desperately, as frequently, as mindlessly – as we did. Partly this was biological difference – they were simply fussier about who they mated with. Because it takes nine months for a woman to make a baby, and nine seconds for a man to make a baby.

Or is that just me?

And of course there was also the cultural injustice. If a boy did it all the time he was Rod Stewart, and if a girl did it all the time she was the Whore of Babylon.

This is what kept sex for the masses so good for so long – the basic principles of supply and demand. Even in the most promiscuous age, heterosexual women were not willing to supply it with the frequency that heterosexual men demanded it. There was once a woman who slept with Roxy Music – all of them, one at a time. But, as far as I am aware, she didn't sleep with anyone from Sweet or the Glitter Band. She had her standards. Traditionally, women – unlike men – were *choosy*. That has changed now, and ushered in the era of junk sex. Sex has become more democratic. Now everybody is a slut.

Dr Emmanuel Katsulis, manager of the Medicare Centre on the Greek island of Crete, has seen at close quarters the mores of young British women when they are on a sun-and-sperm-splashed holiday.

'Each day, around one hundred girls come here to get the morning-after pill,' Dr Katsulis told the *Daily Mirror*. 'Many have slept with three or four boys in a night without using a condom. Mainly, the girls are only about eighteen or nineteen. It's shocking, but it is quite common for British girls to wake up with men they don't know and find themselves unable to remember the night before.'

That's one symptom of junk sex – it was so good, you can't even remember it.

'Last week,' continued Dr Katsulis, 'I had a girl tell me that she'd had sex with three men in one night but had no idea who they were. So she had no choice but to come and get the morning-after pill.'

The old mating rituals of pursuer and pursued are fast disappearing. Now that everyone is a wanton tart, irrespective of gender, standards of sex have declined to the point where the average holiday shag is the sexual equivalent of a Happy Meal.

Junk sex with a series of interchangeable, anonymous, instantly forgettable partners is the only thing on the menu. The tragedy is that a generation of young men and women are growing up with the idea that junk sex is as good as it gets.

Now that restraint is no longer imposed upon men by women, men have to impose it on ourselves. Any man of the world, or indeed any man who has just been around the block a couple of times, knows that not getting laid is far harder than getting laid.

Pop stars are surprisingly restrained. This is because they have endless sexual opportunities and overdose on junk sex before their second record. I once asked a musician who had just been chased down the street by sixty screaming schoolgirls how he avoided having sex with all of them.

'It's easy,' he said. 'Because, when they act like that, I don't feel like the hunter. I feel like the game.'

Young men want as much sex as they can get. In this respect, they resemble middle-aged men and old men. But once you are beyond the city limits of extreme youth, most men prefer to avoid junk sex. Because junk sex is sex without pleasure, without meaning. Junk sex is when you wished you hadn't bothered. The only good thing about junk sex is that you can't remember too much about it.

I had a friend who had a strict 'no tattoos' rule. That is, he did his very best to avoid any sexual encounter with a woman who had tattoos. The way he explained it, sex with a woman who sported a tattoo was just too much like having it off with Popeye. He saw that tattoo and his heart just wasn't in it. The sex was always junk sex.

Then one night he saw a girl who was so lovely – in that leggy, slightly goofy way that fried his slices of unsmoked bacon – that he generously decided to overlook the tattoo that she sported at the top of her thigh. Inevitably, he lived to regret this decision.

For later that night, when they were cojoined in the act of love, with both of them lying on their right side, the woman fore and the man aft – the better to avoid contemplating the tattoo at the top of her thigh – he lifted her long hair and there on the back of her neck was a tattoo of a dragon.

It put him right off his stroke, although – like a marathon runner entering the cheering stadium on wobbly legs – he just about managed to stagger over the finish line. But it was undeniably junk sex and the thing about junk sex is that it is never, ever worth the effort. You shouldn't have to struggle to get over the finish line. You should burst through it with your blood pumping, and an ecstatic gleam in your eye.

It is a scientifically established fact that each generation is more promiscuous than the generation that went before. Back in the sixties, were they all rutting the night away? Of course not. That was the seventies, when any young woman could easily get her hands on the contraceptive pill. Every generation has more sex than the last.

In the eighties, even a seismic cultural shift like AIDS couldn't stop people having sex. AIDS just made eighties kids worry about it more. The dating game continued unabated even through the height of HIV panic. What changed was that young men now spent an abnormal amount of time examining them-selves for early symptoms of a death sentence. And condoms made an unlikely comeback.

In my memory, the eighties were a writhing Roman orgy where people with Princess Diana haircuts and jackets with big shoulders got it on to the sound of Sade's first album. It may have been the time of HIV, but it was also a time of one-night stands. Nothing ever seems to slow the process of increased promiscuity.

So it doesn't matter whether you are twenty-five or fifty-five – I guarantee that the average binge-drinking hoodie is getting it more often than you. But don't envy him. Because what he is having is almost certainly junk sex.

We have all had our share of junk sex. It is part of growing up, part of the process of the boy becoming a man. And junk sex is in some ways a positive experience, because it makes you appreciate real sex with a woman you love. You learn to spot the difference.

The junk sex you have had is with the women whose names, faces and even existence you struggle to recall. That is how you know it was junk sex – it is exactly like junk food. The thing you remember most is how it came and went without leaving much of an impression. As though it possibly never really happened at all.

Junk sex doesn't necessarily mean ships that pass in the night. There was a one-night stand that I shall remember until the day I die – although there is just the one, and it is the only one, if you get my drift. And no doubt there are plenty of married couples who have junk sex – habitual, perfunctory, just-to-be-polite sex.

But junk sex is usually opportunistic, random, an impulse shag. It seems like a good idea at the time, but you discover you are not as famished as you thought. Or as my mum would say when I loaded my plate with more stodge than I could possibly cram into my greedy little cakehole, 'Your eyes are bigger than your belly.' That's junk sex. When you pump it up when you don't really need it, when you don't really feel it. When your eyes are bigger than your belly.

There is a famous old *New Yorker* cartoon where a man in a car is declining the offer of a street-walking prostitute. 'Thanks,' he tells the whore, 'but I was hoping for a trip to the moon on gossamer wings.'

And it is funny because, although we agree it would be good if sex could always be a trip to the moon on gossamer wings, we know that usually it will be a lot more carnal, basic, casual. And that is fine. Casual, basic, carnal can be good. But the modern male should draw the line at junk sex. It is never worth it.

For what a chance we take when we stick that dick into anything other than our underpants. Pregnancy, disease, true love, infidelity – all these things are just an erection away. It is never worth risking all of that on junk sex. When you outgrow the outer limits of your promiscuity, you realise sex should always mean something. Even if it means nothing more than fleeting spasms of pleasure.

And there is no pleasure in junk sex.

I am not suggesting that you should save yourself for the right girl.

But you will have a much happier life if you say no to junk sex, and then recognise her when she comes along.

Sixteen

Tough Girls

Men – have you been beaten up by girls yet? Apparently it is all the rage. When I heard the news, I confess that I felt a twinge of nostalgia for the good old days, when they would get their brothers to beat you up.

But today's modern lass doesn't need her shaven-headed siblings to knock you about. Sisters are doing you by themselves. Women are holding the door open for men – the door to the Accident and Emergency ward.

What happened?

In 2008 87,200 women and girls were nicked for violent assaults. That's 240 every day. That's 10 attacks by women every hour of the year. That's rather a lot.

We are not talking about giving the boyfriend a right-hander in the cakehole. Those 87,200 attacks cover everything from drunken street brawls to muggings to happy slapping to GBH to knife crimes to murder most foul. For the first time in our nation's history, the most common crime among women is violence.

Traditionally, the specialist female crime was theft. A little light shoplifting in Miss Selfridge. That sort of thing. Now they would rather punch your lights out.

You may have missed the Ministry of Justice report. That was the Government's intention. It was slipped out on the Internet after MPs had left for the long summer break, because it was hardly a ringing endorsement of Labour's twenty-four-hour licensing laws.

Round-the-clock drinking was meant to turn us into civilised Europeans, sipping Pernod at a streetside café as we discussed Jean-Paul Sartre's *Les Temps Modernes*. Instead, non-stop boozing has produced a generation of women who are fast becoming as violent as their moronic male counterparts. Give them a bottle of Pernod and they will glass your face.

The term 'fighting like a girl' has come to mean showing an astonishing level of violence matched by a pitiless lack of mercy. Were the young Mike Tyson to appear today, pundits would sigh that 'he fights like a big girl' – and it would be high praise indeed.

Sexual historians will record that fifty years of feminist thought produced men who happily adopted the nobler characteristics of women – committed parenting, emotional openness, a rigorous skin-moisturising regime – while women adopted the very worst traits of their men – binge drinking, falling over and, above all, the willingness to resolve disputes by kicking someone in the ear.

It is not all women, of course. Female violence is a generational thing. It is an economic thing. And it is a class thing.

There are not legions of middle-aged, middle-class women out there saying to their husbands, 'Charles, you *knew* it was your turn to pick up Lucinda from Pony Club – so now I am going to give you a right good hiding, you fucker.'

No, it is not all women. But it is a lot of them. And their numbers are growing.

Female violence is not a minority sport. The violent femmes are the product of a modern age, and an emerging class. They have a few bob, they have a few tattoos, they have a few brain cells. But not very many. Most of all they have an over-whelming sense of entitlement. Why *shouldn't* I be able to do exactly what I want? Drink until I puke. Scream in the street. Vent my spleen until you bleed. Human rights, innit?

Back in the nineties, modern young women used to think they were quite edgy if they got to say, 'Big fat hairy cock,' on late-night Channel 4. How quaint those late twentieth-century new ladettes seem in this age of female violence, as innocent in their big fat hairy cock fixation as your granny with her knitting. Now, heaven knows, anything goes. Possibly one of your eyes.

When an elderly viewer of the *X Factor* recognised one of the contestants as the mugger who had attacked his late wife, the culprit was inevitably one of the girls rather than one of the weepy, wimpy boys.

As the father of a daughter, I am all in favour of girls and women being able to defend themselves. I bought my daughter boxing gloves when she turned five even though she would rather have had a Barbie doll. For one day she will have to put down Barbie and learn how to defend herself.

Before you become the father of girls, you worry that your daughter will meet a man just like you. And then after you become the father of a girl you worry that your daughter will run into a man or men who are infinitely worse than you ever were.

Like any caring, loving, thoughtful father, I want my daughter to be able to rip their balls off and stuff them down their throats.

But I know my daughter's attitude to violence will be primarily defensive. In ten years' time, I don't want her to go out on a Friday night, drink twenty Bacardi Breezers and then assault a nurse in A&E. And that is what is happening with the girls of today – or at least enough of them to fill Wembley Stadium every year. And they are just the ones who are caught. When we talk about modern female violence, it is first-strike stuff – getting their retaliation in first. This is not self-defence. It is lashings of the old ultra-violence, droogy.

Most men have some experience of moderate female violence. It could be argued that no relationship has really got serious until you have had your face slapped, or had a Jimmy Choo thrown at your head.

But in the past – and with the kind of girls who have ruled our world – female violence was almost always an expression of frustration. It was because you had got on her nerves. It was because you had pushed exactly the wrong button at precisely the wrong moment. And it was over as quickly as it had begun.

You just had to guard your vulnerable parts until the storm passed. In extreme cases, you might hold their arms while muttering soothing words of love, although in my experience it was best to let them get it off their chests and try to take it like a man. Or at least without bursting into tears.

The female violence of today is of a completely different order.

The Police Federation puts the blame squarely on licensing reforms, and says that the days when officers could rely on women to be a 'calming influence' are gone. But it is not just the blight of a Happy Hour that lasts for all eternity that has caused female violence.

Yes, booze poured oil on the flames, but they were already burning. Twenty-four-hour drinking was introduced in November 2005, but long before that women had learned to say, 'Come and have a go, if you think you're hard enough.'

Arrests of women for violent offences had been rising steadily for years – almost 70,000 arrests in the year immediately before twenty-four-hour boozing. Binge culture has certainly filled the A&E wards to overflowing. But at the bottom of the social scale, women have been increasingly ready to kick you in the meat and two veg.

Some women commentators have pondered the rise of female violence and concluded that men 'need to get over their notions of the gentler sex'.

Ah, but we can't.

Because we expect women to be inherently better than us.

Nicer. Kinder. And less violent. Wars are started by men. Most murders are committed by men. When a child is abused, sexually or physically, it is usually by a man. Serial killers are men. We can't get over the notion of women as the gentler sex because they are – or at least they always have been. But there was nothing gentle about Chelsea O'Mahoney.

She was jailed for her part in the slaughter of a man called David Morley, beaten to death by a teenage gang while walking home from work. David Morley did not do anything to provoke the attack – but then that goes without saying. Doing nothing can get you killed these days, and not necessarily by men.

The court heard how O'Mahoney laughed as she delivered the final blow to David Morley as he lay dying on the pavement, and in that immortal modern phrase, 'kicked his head like a football'. Before she was caught, Chelsea O'Mahoney also helped to beat to death a tramp sleeping under a railway arch. She enjoyed filming the murders on her mobile phone.

Thirty years ago she would have been stealing lipstick.

In some ways, casual female violence is even more chilling than the front-page murders, because it is becoming such an accepted feature of British culture – a sort of morris dancing for the twenty-first century. The likes of Chelsea O'Mahoney still provoke headlines and op-ed pieces, and they will for a while longer, whereas a couple of daft cows who go ape at 30,000 feet on their way home from a sun-and-sperm package holiday are becoming next to normal.

Two British women, aged twenty-six and twenty-seven, went

on a violent rampage when cabin staff refused to serve them more drink. One woman was heard to shout, 'Let's open the door, I want some fresh air,' before being handcuffed and wrestled to the floor. Student Nathan Sivajoti, eighteen, said, 'They were really loud and foul-mouthed. A family with children asked them to tone down their language. The girls started shouting and it escalated from there. Stewards tried to calm it down. But the worst came when one of them slapped a mum.'

'One was lashing out with a vodka bottle after they were refused more booze,' said another passenger. The flight from Kos had to make an emergency landing in Frankfurt, where the women were escorted off the plane and slung in a cell. The airline that decanted the women – XL Airways – has since gone out of business. But female violence is still booming.

We know these charmers so well, of course – foul-mouthed, pissed out of their tiny brains, demanding respect even as they wave a bottle in your face.

They have been with us for a long time. But in the past they were always men. And now they are women. Female liberation was never meant to be the freedom to behave just as badly as men.

How did we get to this sorry state? You can blame the junk hedonism of our culture. You can blame a state education system that has finally succeeded in producing girls who are every bit as stupid and violent as boys. You can blame the way that, in the buttholes of our major cities, gangs have replaced the family. These factors have all played their wretched part.

But more than anything, I blame the collapse of an old taboo. Not the taboo about women hitting men. The older one. The one where no man worthy of the name ever raised his hand to a woman.

Boys don't hit girls. That's what I was taught. All the girls who ever gave me a smack, or who threw something at me – well, it never even crossed my mind that I was allowed to hit them back. I would no more hit a woman than levitate. And if my father had ever caught me raising a hand to a girlfriend, I have no doubt at all that the old man would have beaten the living daylights out of me.

Quite right too.

But somewhere along the line, the taboo about never hitting women vanished. It was just one of many taboos that died out – like the one about respecting the elderly, or not swearing around children, or not taking more drink or drugs than you could handle. And so we hardly noticed.

But the women on the receiving end of violent men did. So while any government that unleashes a tidal wave of alcohol is dangerously foolish, ultimately I blame men. Who were the men in Chelsea O'Mahoney's life? A rum bunch, I'll warrant.

Men should have remembered. Men should have honoured the taboo. Men should never have raised their hands in violence towards women. The way it was is the way it should be.

Because if women are more violent than they used to be, then that is because second-rate men have made them that way.

Seventeen

A Bigger Cock
Than That

She left me for a man with a bigger cock.

That is what she said (and she said it again and again and again). That was the party line. That was the official version. That was the first line of the press release. *We regret to announce . . . he's got a bigger cock.* And when they tell you that they have left you for a man with a bigger cock, then quite frankly you just have to take their word for it.

You can't argue with a bigger cock. You can't pick a fight with a bigger cock. You can't offer a bigger cock to step outside. You have to hold up your hands and surrender. Don't shoot, bigger cock.

But then – don't they *always* leave you for a man with a bigger cock? At least that's what they say. At least that's what they tell you – and the new guy. Was there ever a woman in the world who said, 'Meet my new boyfriend – he's hung like a hamster next to you.'

A bigger cock. That's what she said. You can imagine my surprise when she later decided she was a lesbian.

Or maybe you can't.

And I thought to myself – Well, yes. Maybe he *did* have a bigger cock and maybe he didn't. And maybe, just maybe – whether he was hung like a horse or a donkey or My Little Pony – *she was just trying to be nasty.*

Because they are, aren't they? It is the hex of the ex. Do you seriously believe that they wish you well, when all the dreams and hopes and plans have turned to ashes? No, she doesn't wish you well. Your ex wishes you hell.

Breaking up is hard to do. But mostly it is hard to do because leaving your life is somehow a licence to be spiteful and snide and cruel. The end comes and you take separate roads and suddenly the love of your life is a thorn in your side. In my experience, the sweetest girl in the world can be the meanest girl in the world – with very little encouragement. All she needs for the transformation is the end of the affair.

I am quite prepared to believe that men are far nastier during a relationship – men are more prone to infidelity, less supportive, less good at the long hard slog of simply being with someone.

But when it is over, then the position is reversed. Women really know how to hurt an ex. Nobody knows how to hurt you like an ex-partner. And all the evidence strongly suggests that there are few things she enjoys more.

Oh, I know some civilised souls stay friends. They shake

hands with the new man and they act as if we are all just inter-changeable bourgeois souls together at one great big cosmic dinner party and it doesn't really matter a damn who you stick your dick in or who you tell 'I love you', or who you build your life around for years and years, or who comes or who goes. Who cares? Let's keep the dinner party polite.

But it was never like that for some of us. I have stayed friendly with lots of women, but they were usually the ones who were only ever really friends in the first place. The casual flings, the holiday romances, the bed buddies. The kind of friends you have sex with.

These women smile when they see me. They are friendly. They give the impression that they actually *like* me. But in my sweet-and-sour experience it is only possible to stay friends with the ones who were no more than friends in the first place.

It is not like that with the real ones. The ones who I built my world around. The five or six big loves that you get *in a lifetime*. The ones that I missed like an amputated limb and who could make the tears come, sudden and unbidden and bitter, years – years! – after it was all over.

Do you think they kiss me on the cheek? Do you think they are as affable as one of the former fuck buddies? Do you think I talk to their new boyfriends and husbands about golf and cars or whatever it is that normal people chitchat about when they bump into their ex and the new guy?

No – they blank me. And I blank them. We walk on by.

And it is as if saying something – even one word! – would open the floodgates of emotion. It is as if saying that one fatal word would cause the dam to break and bring it all back – the good times and the bad, the sheets stained with tears and blood and love, the lost summers and wasted years and shattered dreams.

You know. The good old days.

Also, I have usually run out of affection by then. I am not nostalgic. I don't miss them. Because of the big cock thing or a thousand things just like it. The fact you broke up and they went off with one of your best friends. The fact that they stalk you. Facts like that.

The merciless brutality of the ex never ceases to astound me. It is almost as though they want you to turn love into hate. That old chemical reaction. They will say and do anything – just to see you flinch.

Perhaps women understand something that we do not. Perhaps they know that the only possible way forward is to apply scorched-earth policy to the past. In *The Quiet American*, Graham Greene's hero attempts to survive the end of love by remembering the bad times.

In the moment of shock there is little pain; pain began about three a.m. when I began to plan the life I had still somehow to live and to remember memories in order somehow to eliminate them. Happy memories are the worst, and I tried to remember the unhappy. I was practised. I had lived all

this before. I knew I could do what was necessary, but I was
so much older – I felt I had little energy left to reconstruct.

The stalking, unfavourable cock comparison, sexual revenge
– we can grasp these things. We can comprehend that degree
of emotional violence. What is much harder for a man to understand is the transfer of affection. The way that you are so totally
replaced by . . . just some other guy. Just a pair of trousers that
she picked up in the office or the gym or the bar. Suddenly it
is not you – but *him*.

How did that happen? How does that work? It is not casual
sex. It is not even casual love. You can't call it love. *Generic*
relationship is closer to the mark. What an insult. It would be
so much easier if they left you for the love of their life. Instead
of . . . just some guy.

How they change! If we could see the end then we would
never begin. It is just too bitter, it is just too tough.

I remember the one who said that we would always be
friends. Our friendship would remain, she said – because that
was the important thing – our friendship. That sounded good.

And then, after it became clear that I wasn't the escape route
from her bad marriage, she treated me like a dead man. If you
see me walking down the street . . . treat me like a dead man.
'What happened to our friendship?' I called out one moonlit
night as she walked on by. It was a rhetorical question. And
the next time I saw her, the very next time, she was getting out
of a car with . . . just some guy. And she was pregnant.

That was brutal. It hurt – still does a bit, between you and me, to tell the bitter truth. As if it was not enough for her to move on with her life. As if she wanted to drive it over my life-less corpse.

Graham Greene was right. Remember the bad times. Make the bitter and the bile and the bad memories thrive after the break. And maybe that is what they do. Perhaps that is how she gets over you.

Time after time I have parted ways amicably enough, and then the nastiness has started to creep in. It is often all very friendly at first – that's the irony. Then they rub your nose in their new relationship. Then they start stalking you. Then they start brandishing a bigger cock in a threatening manner.

Very deliberately, they kill the love that remains. You end up happy to be shot of them. You wonder what you ever saw in them. By the time they get into the passive stalking phase – running into you accidentally on purpose, talking up the new guy, hanging around your haunts, trying to impress you with the latest dreary chapter in their empty, desperate lives – you are glad you got out.

Indeed, you are frequently sorry that you ever got in.

Here comes my baby, here she comes now. There she is, just another woman, when for so long I thought she was *the* woman – the only one for me! – knocking on a bit, no spring chicken, a little heavier – aren't we all? – and some new man in tow. Perhaps that is why she seems unrecognisable. The new guy. You see, with all of them, with all of the real ones,

I never thought there would be a new guy. It never crossed my mind.

How dumb can you get?

And the truth is – I prefer it this way. I don't want to be crazy about someone for years and then be just their social acquaintance. I don't want our words of love – talking all night long! – to become small-talk and chitchat. I prefer the white noise of silence. It is a more fitting epitaph to when we were still lovers.

It's a shame. Of course it's a shame. That all those good things went bad. That you crossed the thin line between desire and torment, between love and hate, between being together and being apart.

That suddenly you do not recognise each other.

I mean, often you *literally* do not recognise each other. There are women that I spent years with – women who have measured out my life. And then I have walked past them in the street without recognising their face.

Sometimes it is because they have changed. But it is always more than that – they are someone else now. They have broken the spell. They have become – wonder of wonders – ordinary. When for years I believed with all my heart that they were special.

I suspect that is what hurts most of all. More than what she did with your friend, and more than the passive stalking thing, and certainly more than the whole bigger cock phenomenon.

Love means singling out another human being from the great

mass of humanity. And when they disappear once more into the crowd – when the special becomes ordinary – you know that love has had the last rites. The connection to that special someone has been broken forever. On a planet of seven billion, you are alone again. Licking your wounds and looking for love.

'You're just like her, I'm just like him,' goes the old song. It is the saddest song in the world.

Eighteen

Faulty Modern Men

I do hope you are sitting down, because the breaking news is that you and I are the most pathetic men to ever walk – or shuffle diffidently – across the face of the Earth.

We are a disgrace to our wedding tackle. Unworthy of our meat and two veg. The biggest bunch of pussies in the history of our sex. A source of eternal and infinite shame to our gnarly-faced forefathers, who must be turning in their urns at the sorry state of the neutered modern male.

Are we not men? We are soft lads.

Apparently.

An Australian anthropologist called Peter McAllister has published a book called *Manthropology: The Science of the Inadequate Modern Male* which comes to the painful conclusion that men have now sunk lower than they have ever sunk before.

'The sorriest cohort of masculine homo sapiens to ever walk the planet,' he sniffs. 'If you are reading this then you – or the male you have bought it for – is the worst man in history. No ifs. No buts. The worst man – period.'

Worst? In what way? Less sensitive? More stupid? Less able to control our environment? Less capable of filling in our VAT returns or inspiring a multiple orgasm?

No, when McAllister says we are the worst men, he means we are the *weakest* men. What – mentally? Morally? Spiritually? No, when he says we are the weakest men he means *physically*. Those old-fashioned Neanderthal men were all stronger, faster, harder, tougher and meaner than semi-skimmed, twenty-first-century guy. This is the central point of *Manthropology* – the lamentable physical decline of men.

You might think that Usain Bolt is quite a nippy little runner. But after examining the twenty-thousand-year-old fossilised footprints of an Aboriginal male chasing a kangaroo in New South Wales, McAllister suggests that this unknown hunter was almost as fast. Only almost as fast?

Ah, but he did not have spiked shoes, or a special running track or the promise of glory. This long-lost Aboriginal was not a world-beater, not a record smasher, not an Olympic, multi-gold medallist. He wasn't the fastest man on the planet. He was just Uncle Charlie, chasing his lunch.

Impressive stuff. But is the ability to chase a kangaroo's arse really the way to measure the worth of modern men?

The pitiful decline of modern men goes down particularly well with female newspaper columnists who have been unlucky in love.

'What poor, dead creatures modern men are,' Liz Jones

gleefully lamented in the *Mail on Sunday*. 'What wimps. What wastes of space.'

At least she's not bitter.

Under the headline THE MODERN MALE – HE'S SOFTER THAN A SLUG WITH A BEER BELLY, Liz wrote an eviscerating column about *Manthropology*, using Peter McAllister's book to – metaphorically speaking – club to death every man who had ever disappointed her. And the rest of us.

'Men might all wear trainers and tracksuits and workwear such as denim jeans and combat trousers,' Jones wrote, 'but it is all just dressing up, an illusion, a hark back to the days when men actually knew how to do physical things like, ooh, I don't know, put in a light bulb or change a duvet cover or make love to a woman.'

Liz went on at eloquent, hugely entertaining length about her disgust for the physical state of all modern males. 'Like snails – soft spongy, grey bodies inside the crisp shells of their automobiles . . .' This was strong, shocking stuff, every line vibrating with genuine repulsion. 'Hopelessly soft,' Liz said of modern men, as though it goes without saying that every modern woman has the body of Elle Macpherson.

Any male columnist that wrote about the bodies of women with such open disgust would lose his job. But obesity knows no barriers of gender. Thirty years ago, when I first went to America to frolic with Thin Lizzy along the Eastern seaboard, I was stunned at the fatties waddling down every block. And now you see their porky tribe on any British High Street.

Fat is not a male issue.

It is a people issue.

And what does need pointing out to Liz – and to all the other female columnists who jumped on *Manthropology* with such delight – is that it is very easy to make exactly the opposite case.

Soft bodies? All the men I know are obsessed with going to the gym. Far from conforming to the Liz Jones modern male archetype – 'an arrogant straight bastard who believes, despite the beer gut and nasal hair, he is catnip' – they push their aching bodies to the limit of endurance, sweating their nuts off for that lean, muscled look, then necking their whey protein recovery drinks until it is coming out of their ears. And then doing it all again. And still being tormented by the thought that they do not look anywhere near as good as Ronaldo in his advertisement for pants.

All the men I know are far more obsessed with their health than their fathers and grandfathers ever were. I grew up in a cloud of tobacco smoke, as my dad and uncles merrily smoked themselves into an early grave. Now men are more likely to be killed by overdoing the cardio-vascular exercise.

And exactly where is the evidence that modern man is bad in bed? All the men I know are obsessed with giving their woman pleasure beyond measure – indeed, many of them can't really settle back and enjoy themselves unless the lady has gone through the door first.

This sexual nostalgia for some lost golden age when men were men and women were damn glad of it ignores the undeniable fact that our ancestors did not agonise a whole lot about female satisfaction.

To Granddad, the clitoris was a lot like Croydon. He knew it was somewhere down south, but he did not really care because he had absolutely no plans to ever go there.

'Look at Jamie Oliver,' says Liz. 'A body as soft as butter. Gordon Brown has a body mass index that probably far exceeds the government guidelines. Peter Mandelson? Man boobs. Simon Cowell? Peacock chest and underdeveloped thighs. I could go on. And on.'

And she does. And, yes, she has a point. But Jamie Oliver's love handles and Peter Mandelson's man boobs are no more representative of the modern male than, say, Jenson Button's tight little bottom or Joe Calzaghe's bulging biceps. You can't blame the disappointments caused by the men in your life on all the men in the world.

Or maybe you can.

Like all the best propaganda, this modern man-hating thesis contains a germ of truth.

Yes, of course there are plenty of men about who are unworthy, their bodies and minds slowly decaying from fifty years of peace and prosperity, good for nothing but putting on their snow-white trainers and watching Internet porn and the Premiership. Yes, there are guys like that, and Liz Jones seems to have gone out with a few of them.

But in all the ways that count, the strong, silent majority of men are far better than they have ever been.

Noble of heart. Quick of mind. Steely of resolve. Stiff of rod. And though we might not be able to hunt a wild animal quite as nimbly as Uncle Charlie did back in the Bush of twenty thousand years ago, there is nothing remotely inadequate about the modern man. Look at us, will you?

We fulfil the traditional male roles of providing for and protecting the ones we love. And yet we embrace the new male roles – sharing our feelings, staying awake after sex and – crucially – parenting.

From the blissfully happy moment of their birth – which we would not dream of missing – the men of today are involved in raising their sons and daughters in a way that would have been unthinkable even thirty years ago.

What more do they want from us?

We watch what we eat. We go to the gym. We go out into the working world to make money for our families. We are considerate lovers. We read bedtime stories to our nippers. If there is a noise downstairs in the night, we go downstairs to investigate with a baseball bat. These are the actions of mature, well-rounded, fulfilled and loving men. Or would they rather we were really good at grabbing a kangaroo's arse?

Inadequate?

Who are you calling inadequate?

*   *   *

The cover of *Manthropology* features the six stages of the evolution of men.

There's a hunched up little monkey man. Then a monkey man who has learned to stand up straight. Then a slightly larger monkey man who has had his body waxed – sack, back and crack, as they say in the beauty parlours. Then a heavily muscled man – hardly a monkey at all – sporting a big beard. And then the star of our species – a naked gladiator with big biceps, a big shield and an even bigger sword. Look at the size of that thing!

And finally, oh dear – there's poor old modern man. A flabby man-boobed slob, hunched over his palm-held device. You and me.

Except that is not you and it is not me, is it?

I mean, we all play with our hand-held devices from time to time – oh, stop sniggering – but it is hardly the whole picture. It is not even a snapshot. It is not even the frame.

'Every generation is softer than the one that came before,' my father always told me when I was growing up. And it hurt. Because I knew – measuring myself against my father, which was the only way I knew of gauging my worth – it was true.

At the age when I was doing amphetamine sulphate with The Clash, my father was killing Germans. Of course, I couldn't physically compare to my dad. He made John Wayne look like Kenneth Williams.

When he died at the age of sixty-two, my dad could still
have kicked my butt with both hands tied behind his back. But
I found that I could do other things. Good things. I found them
in work. I found them in loving someone. I found them in being
a father. And by being a different kind of father to my own.

My dad killed Nazis – dozens of the bastards. I could never
compete with that. I could never be my father. And I could
never get the killer's glint that my dad got in his eye at the first
sign of trouble.

But I did what we must all do.

I found a different kind of manhood.

I found other ways to be a man.

The author of *Manthropology* misses the obvious – men need
a different set of tools today.

Running fast will not pay your mortgage. Jumping high will
not get you that job. And your ability to arm wrestle will not
win you a mate – unless of course you are in a really rough
bar.

It is fine getting all sentimental about the men of the distant
past. But what this Australian academic doesn't tell you is that
Neanderthal Uncle Charlie probably died when he was an old
man of twenty-six. Struck down by the pox. Bit by a rabid
kangaroo. Breaking a leg while out hunting for brunch and
then starving to death, the silly bugger. Could it possibly be
that is why men are softer than they were twenty thousand years

ago? Because as we evolved we discovered that being hard is just not enough.

'Men no longer chase wildebeest across the pampas,' claims Liz Jones, 'and therefore have become hopelessly soft.'

In fact, the modern male probably retains a few too many of the old ways for his own good. The need to hunt, the desire to fight and the endless impulse to spill his seed. It doesn't make for a quiet life. That is why the modern man often seems a troubled soul. Not because he has grown so soft. But because he retains so many of the old ways.

'Honestly,' says Liz Jones, 'the number of times I have wanted to exclaim, while prone: "For God's sake, put your back into it, man!"'

Ah, but that's not modern men, Liz. That's just your ex-boyfriends.

Don't ask the rest of us to carry their dismal little cans.

Nineteen

Get Fit with Fred

He did not look like other men.

He was running down our street early on a rainy Saturday morning and everything about the man set him apart. He ran with this lazy, high-stepping gait and his kit was odd – tight black leggings, a yellow rain slicker that you might wear if you were fishing for cod on the North Sea, and a long-brimmed baseball cap pulled low over his handsome face. And he was lean – not a gram of wasted flesh on him, lean in a way that men are no longer lean. There was an animal grace about him – he made you think of a panther, and the fact that he was black did not come into it.

'My God,' I said to my wife as we drove past him on the otherwise deserted North London street. 'That guy looks fit.'

'Yes,' said my wife. 'That's because that guy is Thierry Henry.'

Before a certain age – twenty-five – a man can get away with anything. No amount of lager will give you one too many chins.

No stash of recreational drugs shall wither the under-twenty-fives, nor junk food steal the rosy glow of their cheeks.

In youth, there are two things you never think about: you do not think about diet, and you do not think about dying. But the immortal cockiness of youth does not last long. It is gone before you know it, before you have really had a chance to appreciate it. The wrong side of twenty-five and you wear your diet, and your drinking habits, and your exercise – or lack of it – on your face and in your waistband.

Even hard-living young men who are still in their twenties – off the top of my head, I think of Pete Doherty, I think of Prince Harry – suddenly get a puffiness about them, a softness of feature that is the legacy of all that fun in the wee small hours of the morning. So soon Harry's cocktails at Funky Buddha start to show! So soon the smack asks Pete to come up with the bill!

Long, long before a man reaches his thirtieth birthday, he must make an active choice.

Do you want to be fat?

Or do you want to be fit?

We can't all look like Thierry Henry. But that doesn't mean you have to look like Henry VIII.

You can't do much about your male pattern baldness – what pattern did you think you were going to get? – and you can't stop the ageing process.

But you can stop the fat bastard process.

Male breasts – when did they become so popular? I don't mind getting old. I don't mind developing diseases that will numb my brain or weaken my body or make my knob drop off. Time and fate will see to that.

But I refuse to grow a pair of breasts. I refuse – will not permit it – to start looking like Tony Blair flashing his décolletage in a borrowed holiday villa. We can't do anything about growing old, but we can do everything about growing fat. Follow the example of the great Bill Shankly. Plan to die a fit man.

Going to the gym – what's that? Sitting around in your shorts watching MTV? Parking yourself by the free weights and eyeing the girls in their lycra? Telling the guys in the locker room what you did at the weekend?

If you want to be truly fit, fitter than you have ever been, fit for life, fit for anything, then don't go to a gym. Go to a trainer.

I found Fred Kindall and lost a stone in one year. I found him where the music played – in the semi-secret North London gym above a Bagel Street where the soundtrack is The Clash, The Specials, The Upsetters, The Maytals, The Wailers, The Jam, The Skatalites, Delroy Wilson and Joni Mitchell.

Joni Mitchell? That's how tough it is in Fred's gym. That's how butch. We are so macho that sometimes we put on a bit of Joni Mitchell while we are whaling on the heavy bag with

our eighteen-ounce Lonsdale sparring gloves. We even have a
pink skipping rope.

It's all deliberately provocative – like walking into the meanest
bar in Dodge City on a Saturday night and ordering a glass
of milk. Yeah – that's right, stranger. The song you hear is from
Joni Mitchell's *Blue* album.

You got a problem with that?

Going to the gym is for Mister Softies. Going to the gym is for
fat boys who want to kid themselves they are getting fit. If you
are serious about getting in shape, then you don't go to a gym.
You go to Fred. Or someone just like Fred.

'You're so lucky to be training!' Fred shouts at me as I throw
a long, loping right hook at his body armour. 'It's good to be
alive!'

Fred has many catchphrases. He is like Bruce Forsyth. I
expect him to say, Nice to punch you, to punch you – nice!

But he says something else.

'Pain is just weakness leaving the body,' says Fred.

Boys buy condoms and don't use them. Men buy exercise equip-
ment and don't use it. The spirit is willing, and the Nike shorts
are good looking, but when it comes to climbing on the ellip-
tical trainer for an hour, we are so weak.

Now more than ever, men want to be the best that they

can be. We know that it is only the poor and the ignorant who are fat. There are so many things in this world that we cannot control. But no man has to live with breasts.

For the first time in human history, heterosexual men look at pictures of other heterosexual men and say, 'Wow, look at the abdominal muscles on *that.'*

'If Kurt Cobain had played football,' Damon Albarn said at the height of Brit Pop, 'then he would never have killed himself.'

Albarn was mocked for the statement at the time – the Blur singer's sudden passion for football being seen as another ludicrous working-class affectation, to go alongside visits to the dog track, wearing vintage Sergio Tacchini tops and hanging out with Phil Daniels.

But Damon was right – the man who has any kind of physical life is unlikely to throw away that life in a fit of dark despair.

To embark on any course of serious exercise is to subject yourself to a life of low-level yet almost constant pain – of knocks and strains and aches and bruises and little wounds that will not heal, of rest days when you feel so tired that you can hardly climb the stairs, of endless three-minute rounds – punching, crunching, spinning – where you can't help but remember your old friend Douglas Adams, dropping dead in a gym in Los Angeles.

But you never doubt that you have a life, and that it is worth living, and the endorphins produced by hard physical exercise are guaranteed to be the best drug you ever tasted.

Training is a chemical experience you are likely to become addicted to, for the properties of endorphins are similar to those of opiates. That is what finding your own private Fred will do for you – everything will hurt like hell but you will feel great.

Damon Albarn was right. If Kurt Cobain had gone for a kickabout with Oasis and Blur, he would still be alive today.

But he would probably have had to go in goal.

For the first half of my twenties, I abused my body in every way imaginable, and a few that are unimaginable. There was a period – strange to recall, as I heat up my porridge oats (the breakfast of champions) every morning – when I had amphetamine sulphate for breakfast. And it wasn't even high-fibre amphetamine sulphate.

That kind of life can't last, and you would not want it to.

When I was a young man, most of the people I knew who died brought it on themselves. Heroin usually, with a side order of cocaine. But now, decades later, cancer and heart disease have come calling on blameless, innocent souls and death is just the luck of the draw.

Training does not stop the long slow slide to the grave, but it makes it more of a fun ride. Few things in life give me as much pleasure as trying to punch a hole in Fred's body armour, even though I know I never will.

And I have realised that I can't do it alone. I don't want to be another fat, middle-aged guy eyeing the lovelies over his beer-and-carbs gut, but without Fred to drive me on I might be.

Any honest description of Fred makes him sound like the training instructor in *Full Metal Jacket*, and indeed there is something of the fanatic about him. But like any great trainer, he knows that there are off days – when you have been out on the town, when you have been working for seven days straight, when you are carrying an injury – and sometimes a change is needed to the regime.

That's what a Fred does for you – he keeps you training when the guys that play park football at the weekend are sitting on the sidelines with their crocked knees and ankles.

And as the sergeant prepares the boys for Vietnam in *Full Metal Jacket*, so you need a Fred to push you to the limit – wherever that might be. Under your own steam, you will not get anywhere near your limit. Because getting to your limit is totally against human nature. You will be kind to yourself. You will see sense. You will be reasonable. You will cop out.

To train – to really train – you need a Fred. I have been lucky. For years I had a brilliant Kung Fu *sifu* called David Courtney Jones, and then later I followed the music to that mythical gym, and I found Fred. And between those two trainers, when I was doing it alone – getting on the old ski machine, running in the park, going to the gym and sitting on my can to stare at MTV – I could not stand to look at myself in the mirror.

And then, after a few years with Fred, my trousers no longer knew me. They didn't fit. None of them. Too baggy. They all had to be thrown away. At an age when my contemporaries were squeezing into their dead man's cords and circus tent chinos, I was contemplating getting the kind of sprayed-on strides last seen on Amy Winehouse.

And then I did.

And I looked bloody ridiculous.

Thierry Henry running in the rain. It was a beautiful sight, and I wondered what he was doing on the street where we lived.

It was the end of the year and this neighbourhood, this city, was over for him. He had left Arsenal, left London, and his marriage had ended. No doubt he was back in Hampstead to see his daughter, and yet his sudden appearance in the rainy mist seemed magical, it had the quality of a dream.

But it is so easy for us to stand back and admire the Thierry Henrys – the men who somehow seem more than men. It is so easy for us to think that physical excellence is beyond the reach of mere mortals like you and me, so easy to think that sport is Andy Gray's post-match analysis, so easy to get fat, get lazy, get breasts.

Refuse to go quietly. Do not go gently into that comfy sofa. For you can tell in a second the men who train and the men who do not, the men who have their own private Fred and those who have let themselves become so soft and flabby and milky that they hardly qualify as men at all.

You will still die. Time will still keep slipping. One day you will cry – *Mirror, mirror, on the wall – I am my father, after all.* The male pattern baldness will not suddenly take on a more fetching pattern. But there is no shame in growing old or bald. There is only shame in growing male boobs.

So find your Fred. Follow the sound of 'The Guns of Navarone'. Forget 'working out' and 'going to the gym' and 'exercising'.

And start training.

'It makes your cock harder,' says Fred, and I duck as he throws a stiff left jab at my head. 'It's so good to be alive!'

It beats the alternative.

Twenty

Gentlemen, Please

Being a gentleman has nothing to do with class. It has nothing to do with clothes. It has nothing to do with etiquette, status or style – unless it is a deep style, the values that define your life, and the stuff that is always there in your blood and bones, the indefinable thing that makes you recoil at anything that insults your soul.

The gentleman – he sounds like an old-fashioned guy, an outmoded concept from some late, unlamented social hierarchy. And yet we need him more than ever, this man who aspires to be good, to be better, to be the best he can be.

But what the world needs now is a model that will work in our own time – a gentleman capable of knowing what makes a man a man in the twenty-first century. And it's not about what knife you use, or how you knot your tie, or when to dare to open the door for the other sex.

The new model gentleman will have to carry himself with a manly bearing in a world of economic collapse, mass un-employment and disposable masculinity.

He works – if he has a job – in a world where women are,

at the very least, his equals. He lives on a planet where the darker angels of our nature are on the rise – racism, xenophobia, political extremism. When the world is increasingly dog eat dog and cat eat mouse, charm is not enough. The new model gentleman knows that the world does not revolve around his cravat.

But with all the certainties of the last century in freefall, the gentleman will do the right thing. Or at least he will strive to do the right thing. And if he fails, then he will know that he has failed.

In this respect the new model gentleman will be like his ancestors. The gentleman of any age has an awareness that forever separates him from lesser men. But this is no longer to do with education, rank or birth. It is a raised consciousness, a hard-earned awareness of when something is wrong. One of the most perceptive definitions of what makes a man a gentleman came, inevitably enough, from the son of a fish-market porter and a charlady.

'A gentleman is never *unintentionally* rude,' said Michael Caine.

This awareness should not be confused with self-consciousness. A real gentleman would not waste time fretting about the amount of his shirt cuff visible to the watching world. But he knows when something is right. And if he insults someone, it is because he intended to, and because they deserved it. It is all about standards.

*   *   *

'Take off your hats,' he said, and the other two men looked at him, not quite getting it, and slowly realising that the speaker – the man alone, the gentleman in the corner –was ready to take it to the next level.

Wherever that level might be.

But only if they were stupid enough to keep their hats on.

The gentleman had been alone in the lift. The other two men – two loud city boys in hats – had entered and continued their conversation. It was office banter of a sexual nature. The solitary gentleman smiled. But when an older woman got into the lift on the next floor, the gentleman noticed that the sexual banter was still being broadcast at the same volume. And now he stopped smiling.

'Take off your hats.'

In the end the gentleman did it for them. He removed their hats. He gave them their hats. The conversation made an emergency stop. The two men were not quite sure what had happened. Or what was happening. Or what was at stake.

But as their sexual banter fizzled out, they knew it had nothing to do with hats.

The scene was almost a throwaway vignette in the second series of *Mad Men*. In telling them to take off their hats, Don Draper was not playing the hard man or the prude. For being a gentleman is not about being tougher or prissier than the next guy. It is not about hard men or prudes.

But it is about being right, and knowing what is right, and having an awareness of inappropriate behaviour so acute that you are prepared to take a beating, if that is what it comes to.

Don Draper represents more than nostalgia for lean-boned, sharp-suited, good-looking masculinity. He embodies the profound longing that many of us feel for a time when men were better than they are today. When being a gentleman was as profound as religion, as private as prayer, and as inseparable from a man as the colour of his eyes.

Something has been lost.

Men are not what they were and it has less to do with the reasons generally advanced – the lack of righteous wars, the death of traditional industry, the rise of women in the workplace – than a kind of collective amnesia.

When did we deteriorate into a bunch of whining crybabies who never lift anything heavier than a BlackBerry? Men have forgotten what we should expect and demand from ourselves. Men have got soft.

And yet here is the bitter irony – as a gender we have never been more thug-like, never more inclined to disrespect women, children and the old.

Never less like gentlemen.

All the old taboos – the ones about expecting men to respect those who are physically, socially or financially weaker than they are – are dying in the dust.

But a gentleman knows. He has a desire to provide and

protect and yet he is not defined by his job, his wage packet or the size of his biceps.

The gentleman has a natural selflessness, an understated altruism – towards his children, towards those less fortunate than himself.

The gentleman is no plaster saint. But his code – his life, his existence – is defined by what he considers appropriate behaviour.

The values that he embodies – decency, the willingness to do whatever he can for the weak, the vulnerable, the underdog – physically, financially, whatever it takes – these are not old-fashioned values, but eternal.

And it follows that, if he wishes to be true to his code, he must sometimes – when he sees a woman being disrespected, when he hears inappropriate language in front of a child – be prepared to clean someone's clock.

Even if he is outnumbered.

Even if he fails.

Especially then.

The way a gentleman acts is not defined by the chances of success, but by what is right.

In a world where manhood is often derided, where advertising depicts fathers and husbands and boyfriends as global village idiots, the gentleman still carries himself with a manly bearing.

He is the light that never goes out.

*   *   *

The new model gentleman is a different breed from the ghosts of gentlemen past.

But then the gentleman has never been a static figure, he has constantly evolved to suit his changing world.

Over the past five hundred years, the etymology of 'the gentleman' has moved from his coat of arms to the size of his heart, from an emphasis on rank to a stress on personal qualities.

And although the term is derived from the French *gentilhomme* – nobleman – the new model gentleman is as likely to have gone to the local comprehensive as Eton.

When MPs were caught with their snouts in the trough of the public purse, the gluttony for free money cut across all political and class barriers. Base human nature in all its greed was no stranger to either council estate or country estate. But if anything, the old school Tories – the ones who would have been quickest to call themselves 'gentlemen' – were the worst of the bunch, with their claims for cleaning moats and building duck houses.

They may be toffs. But they are not gentlemen.

Yet that has been true for almost a hundred years, ever since a generation of privately educated, suicidally brave young officers led their men out of the trenches in the Somme and Ypres and Verdun.

Those doomed, beautiful boys were toffs. And they were gentlemen too.

But the upper class can no longer be relied upon to provide

the world with gentlemen. We must seek nobility elsewhere. We must find it in ourselves.

The gentleman strides across the moral wasteland of our times. He looks good, because he is a man of taste, and yet the gentleman can care about clothes without making them his master. There are higher things. You've got to be true to your code. In the office, in the bedroom, in an unfair world. The values you hold dear are fashion-proof. A gentleman is not his wardrobe.

I suspect that this yearning to be a gentleman secretly exists in the heart of many a modern male – to find a better way to think, to act and to be a man. The very concept of the gentleman sounds a hopelessly archaic concept. And yet in our bones we know that, in these new hard times, we need him more than ever – to give manhood meaning, to find a creed we can believe in.

The gentleman's time has come again. And this time round, perhaps he will not be terrified if he should say loo or lavatory or toilet.

Like King Arthur sleeping until Avalon calls him in her hour of greatest need, so the gentleman has waited until modern manhood faced its darkest night to be reborn.

Because, above all, the gentleman believes that being a man means something.

The gentleman places his faith in a world where manhood is still something good, decent and true. Something worth fighting for. And something to be proud of.

Twenty-One

How to Be Happy

Do you wish it could be Christmas every day? Or would that happy dream quickly turn into the Seventh Circle of Hell?

Being locked in a room with relatives you don't like and food you don't need and presents you don't want – not for one special day but for all of dreary eternity – would that really make you happy? But if a universe where it is forever Christmas wouldn't make you happy, then what would? What does it take for us to be happy?

For centuries man scrabbled and fought and clawed for survival. You don't worry about being happy when the next-door neighbours are keeling over with the Black Death. You don't ponder the nature of true happiness when the Luftwaffe is dropping bombs on your granny. But survival is no longer the issue. In fact, these days we are a bit miffed that we ever have to die at all. And so, as we live our lush lives under the godless heavens, we turn to man's final question – how to be happy?

Is it better to elbow our way to the peak of the working world or leave the rat race behind? Should we spread our seed

far and wide or save it for hearth and home? Should you love
your fellow man or look after number one?

Do we learn to count our blessings? Or should we strive
without ceasing for the nicer life, the bigger house, the better
job, the faster car, the prettier woman, all the gilded laurels of
the big boys. But when to stop? And would you be happy then?

Nothing haunts the modern male like this conundrum – When
will I be happy? There is even a name for it – Hedonics, the
branch of psychology that concerns itself with the study of
pleasant and unpleasant sensations, and what ultimately makes
us happy.

We think we know what it takes, but we soon learn that
we know nothing. Happiness is more than an upgrade in job,
car or home. Happiness is more than the absence of pain.
Happiness is more than a moment of transient bliss. We confuse
Hedonics – that which gives us pleasure – with hedonism – the
pursuit of pleasure as a matter of principle. And though the
terms spring from the same root, they are light years apart. It
is the difference between taking quiet joy in the odd glass of
Merlot and believing you should get rat-faced every night.

We think that the recipe for instant happiness is – stuff it all
in. All the lovers you can bed, all the drink you can hold down,
all the fast white powder you can shovel up your greedy snout.
But hedonism is merely the desperate flight from unhappiness.

We're like Phil in *Groundhog Day* – the film that, more than
any other, defines modern man's struggle towards enlightenment – who, upon discovering that he is stuck in the same day

forever, decides to indulge every appetite. For Phil, it is cream cakes, but it could just as easily be Bacardi Breezers or crack cocaine or Russian hookers.

And it doesn't work.

Too much of a good thing leads to abject – and almost instant – misery. But if the things we want will not make us happy, then what the hell will?

In *Groundhog Day*, Phil only begins to take his tentative steps towards true happiness when he turns away from selfish, fleshy, cream-and-jam pleasures and learns to devote himself to others – the choking diner, the boy falling from a tree, the homeless man, who in the end he cannot save. Phil is only set free when he learns to love, truly love, Andie MacDowell – and not just try to trick her into dropping her pants.

Groundhog Day has been called the most spiritual movie of all time, because it shares a message endorsed by many religions – in the end, the only thing that will still your restless, anxious heart is the peace that comes with loving others.

And yet, unless you are Nelson Mandela, that feels like a very fragile kind of happiness. What if Phil's girl had run off with the nerdy cameraman? What should he do then? Give the cream cakes and the gluttony another shot? If selfishness has its limits, then surely selflessness does too. Being Shaun Ryder might not make you happy. But would being Jesus Christ really be that much better?

In America they now teach happiness at Ivy League

universities. The most popular course at Harvard is run by Dr Tal Ben-Shahar, whose sales pitch is irresistible – for he believes that you can actually learn to be happy.

Dr Ben-Shahar says in his book *Happier – Learn the Secrets to Daily Joy and Lasting Fulfilment* that we should think of our route to happiness as being akin to ordering a hamburger.

There is the rat-race hamburger, which would be a healthy vegetarian burger – it tastes like crap but hopefully does you some good in the long run, like the man who flogs himself to death at work hoping for a happier tomorrow.

Then there is the hedonist hamburger, which is pure junk, stuffed with sugar and salt aplenty – tastes yummy when it is going down but leaves you sick and depleted, like the man who lives his life gorging on pleasure, trying not to think about how he will feel in the morning.

Then there is the nihilist hamburger, which tastes horrible and does you absolutely no good and for dessert you slash your wrists – the standard fare of the man who has lost his lust for life, taking no pleasure in his present and allowing no hope for the future.

And finally there is the happiness hamburger, which tastes good and does you good – like the man who is content with his today and looking forward to tomorrow.

But that is exactly the hamburger that is so rarely on the menu, and we spend our lives constantly getting our order wrong – lost in the quick kicks of hedonism as young men, then lost on the work treadmill as older men, and finally losing faith in the whole sad game as we slip into the mute nihilism of our later years.

'The rat racer becomes a slave to the future; the hedonist a slave to the moment; the nihilist a slave to the past,' writes Tal Ben-Shahar. 'Happiness is not about making it to the peak of the mountain nor is it about climbing aimlessly around the mountain. Happiness is the experience of climbing towards the peak.'

But what if your rope breaks?

Dr Ben-Shahar stresses that happiness will always be out of reach if you expect it to arrive after achieving one burning ambition. Get this job and I will be happy. Go to bed with this woman and I will be happy. Buy this big house and I will be happy. It doesn't work like that, insists the Harvard professor, who as a teenager achieved his ambition of becoming a national squash champion in his native Israel and then slipped into crushing depression.

If our wants and needs are fulfilled, he insists, we are not full men. We are empty shells. A state where our desires have all been met is a wasteland. Goals are the key to happiness, says Dr Ben-Shahar.

'The primary purpose of having a goal is to enhance enjoyment of the present,' he writes. 'The goals need to be meaningful and the journey they take us on needs to be pleasurable for them to bring about a significant increase in happiness.'

But what goals should we pursue? To give ourselves whole-heartedly to the search for love or give our all in the struggle for the legal tender? Should we worry about our health or never worry about it at all? Should we spend quality time with our family or avoid them whenever decently possible? Somehow we know that, if we are to be happy, fully-formed men then we have to care about others, both our loved ones and people we will never meet.

We can all see the truth in Woody Allen's line, 'If I know that just one person is starving, then it takes the shine off my whole day.' But we also have hungers and thirsts of our own, and we know that they will still be there when the last starving man has been allowed to eat his fill.

If we are to avoid eventual bitterness and disappointment, then our goals in the material world need to be realistic and the rewards hard-earned. And even then your six-figure bonus will turn to dust in your hands if other parts of your life are a wreck. What good is being a big swinging dick in the working world if your partner loves someone else or if your children hate you or if you have just discovered a tumour the size of the Ritz?

Love, success, health – these are all prerequisites of happiness, but they do not get you to your final destination. They just allow you to collect your boarding card. And you will never get there until you learn to count your blessings. The foundation of true and lasting happiness is built on many things, but above all it is knowing when you have got it good – and that you could have it a lot worse.

A survey by psychologist Robert Biswas-Diener revealed that the prostitutes in the backstreets of Calcutta were actually quite a happy little band, because they were relieved that they were not among the thousands of crippled beggars who spent every day of their lives crawling and clawing their way through the filthy streets.

Jonathan Haidt, a social psychologist and author of *The Happiness Hypothesis: Putting Ancient Wisdom and Philosophy to the Test of Modern Science,* believes (although he is personally every inch the academic liberal) it is old-fashioned conservative values that make us happy.

Tradition. Ritual. Family values. The work ethic. A suit and tie. The underrated pleasures of an ordered life are the thing, says Dr Haidt. For when anything goes, we end up like sugar-crazed, hyperactive, unhappy children, weepy and wired and wanting only to go home.

What links all the high priests of happiness is their emphasis on balance, especially the balance between opposed principles. The balance between long-term goals and immediate needs. The balance between self-interest and social altruism. The balance between your potential and your limitations. The balance between family and work, love and sex, me time and their time, delayed gratification and the needs of right here, right now.

In Ken Grimwood's fantasy novel *Replay*, a man is given his chance to live his life again and again, repeatedly dying at the age of forty-two and being reborn in his teenage skin. He does things differently every time, but nothing brings him happiness, because he never achieves anything remotely resembling balance.

At first he pays too much attention to getting rich and neglects his personal life. Then in his next lifetime he devotes too much of himself to social status, and ends up in a cold, loveless marriage with a wife who despises him. Only at the end, when it is too late, when there are no more lives to be led, does he find peace, and something resembling happiness, when he learns to love the moment he is living in. And perhaps that is the best any of us can hope for.

Happiness is not a permanent state. You can't suddenly and unexpectedly arrive there, as though it was a destination just beyond the edge of the A to Z. Even with all the stalwarts in place – the work going well, the doctor's tests all clear, the money coming in, the family happy, the sun shining – happiness comes and happiness goes, and the heartbreaker is that we so rarely appreciate it when we are up to our necks in it.

A survivor of the Bataan death march said how he never focused on surviving as a prisoner of the Japanese, or living through the war, or even through the day. His goal was to put one exhausted foot in front of the other, and just *make it to the next rock.*

That's a pretty good definition of happiness – knowing what you can reasonably ask of yourself.

And then making it to the next rock.

Twenty-Two

New Man, Old Lad

Google the New Man and he comes stumbling forth like a character from the mists of history – soft and self-deprecating, a neutered fossil, an emasculated relic, nervously hiking up his paisley boxer shorts, apologetic about the sins of men, real and imagined, apologetic about existing.

Remember the New Man? As a response to thirty years of feminism, the New Man was as historically inevitable as the collapse of Communism, or John Prescott taking up croquet, or Robbie Williams becoming a fat bastard.

Some things are just written in the stars.

The New Man was what happened when old man started to look horribly dated. When the old ways of being a man no longer worked, the New Man was what ordinary men were meant to aspire to – the poster boy for a more enlightened age, an infinitely more thoughtful chap than his fumbling forebears. Sensitive. Supportive. And softer – much softer – than the men of the past.

The New Man was the fantasy figure of late twentieth-century feminist thinking, the pin-up boy of a new, improved non-macho male world. And the reason that he never really caught on was because he was never real.

Real men were never ever like the New Man, even if they had changed in the final few decades of the twentieth century. And we had all changed, because now we knew that parenting meant us too, and because many of us worked alongside more women than men, and because we had realised that having a second wage packet coming into the house didn't automatically make our cocks drop off – that only happened when she could boast about having a much bigger one than you (we are still talking about wage packets).

But real men never changed enough to make the New Man any more than wishful thinking.

The New Man was an unrealistic proposition because his existence insisted on the total and utter feminisation of men. There was a very corny but spectacularly successful Athena poster that summed up the New Man. In the poster a shaven-chested hunk cradled his baby boy in his muscular arms with all the tenderness of a woman, of a mother.

The mistake was to assume that a man could hold his child with such love, such care, such infinite sensitivity and therefore have absolutely no inclination to take the au pair from behind as she was emptying the dishwasher.

The New Man was strangled at birth because he was always too good to be true.

And yet the instinct to redefine manhood, masculinity and

everything never died. Because now the question was in our heads – *What does it mean to be a man?*

Americans in particular drove themselves nuts trying to answer the question. In the States there was actually a masculine movement – now who would want to join that? A masculine movement sounds like something you have after a large bowl of Alpen.

Unlike feminism, the masculine movement produced no great writers, no great books. The men couldn't produce their own Germaine Greer or Gloria Steinem. There was nothing as totemic as *The Female Eunuch* to rally around. Robert Bly wrote a book called *Iron John*, which argued that the traditional images of manhood were exhausted, and that men should seek alternatives in mythology, folklore and legend. But that kind of hi-faluting stuff was never going to resonate with the man on the New Jersey Turnpike, or the M25.

Feminism was a mainstream cultural event – it might have begun with intellectuals like Germaine Greer, but in the end it touched the life of every housewife, every schoolgirl, every female in the developed world. The male equivalent was always the preserve of academics and poets like Robert Bly, who mostly sought the path of inoffensive machismo, and it never broke out of campus, or made it back from the woods.

But even if we were not hugging each other in the woods, there was no denying that the question of what it means to be a man was in the heads of every man with an IQ higher than his golf handicap.

In this country, the response was more realistic, more measured, more cynical, and came to a defining moment one day in
1991 when the writer Sean O'Hagan sat down and wrote a
massively influential – and even more massively misunderstood –
article about what it means to be a man in our time.

O'Hagan's piece was called, 'Here Comes the New Lad'.

The way Sean told it, the New Lad was, 'a rather schizoid,
post-feminist fellow with an inbuilt psychic regulator that enables
him to imperceptibly alter his consciousness according to the
company he keeps. Basically, the New Lad aspires to New
Man status when he's with women, but reverts to Old Lad type
when he's out with the boys. Clever, eh?'

Very clever. And any modern man who read Sean O'Hagan's
essay had no difficulty at all in saying – God, that's me.
Sensitive, enlightened, caring – but only up to a point, and the
point was where you had to surrender your manly soul.

Every man who read O'Hagan's treatise on the New Lad
had known nothing but girls and women who had been shaped
by decades of feminism – and so we had been touched by it
too. And we were even broadly sympathetic to its aims, as long
as we could still go to the football on a Saturday afternoon,
and as long as all the stuff we really liked wasn't suddenly seen
as symbolic of an oppressive, patriarchal society.

O'Hagan put a name to something that had existed for
years – the way men had learned to accommodate female
thought in the home, in the workplace, in our hearts – while
still remaining essentially true to the old ways.

Are we not men? We are New Lads.

Tragically, all this was way too deep for the average thicko, but they loved the phrase – *the New Lad* had a real ring to it, and very soon it came to mean a revival of old-fashioned yobbism. Liam Gallagher farting in bed, basically, and pop stars in football shirts, and men who were beer-swilling, biscuit-eating, effing-and-blinding Neanderthals.

But when Sean O'Hagan coined the phrase, that wasn't remotely what he was on about. The New Lad, said Sean, had actually read *The Female Eunuch*. 'Among unavailable women or in mixed, convivial company, he has a tendency to overstate his non-sexist sensibilities to the point where the women present don't get a word in.'

All that was soon right out the window, and the vision was hijacked to mean that being a New Lad was in fact exactly like being an Old Lad. Now the question of *What does it mean to be a man?* never arose. Instead there was just a licence for bad behaviour.

O'Hagan had said that the New Lad should have been 'the best a man can get', but it came to mean the worst a boy can be. Being a New Lad meant never having to say, 'Have you come yet?'

Yet the dream lives on to find a third way, a way to be neither New Man wimp nor New Lad oaf, to be true to the manly virtues while respecting our women. Has the time of the New New Man come at last?

There will never be a male equivalent of *The Female Eunuch* to point the way forward, or tell us how far we have come. Men will never form a movement for that would go against the way we are, deep down in our competitive, lone-wolf souls. But if the New New Man flies solo, that doesn't mean he cares nothing for his brothers.

The New Man flopped because he tried to pretend that men had changed completely. The New Lad – in his belching, farting, 'More tea, Vicar?' incarnation – failed because he tried to pretend that men had never changed at all.

The New New Man knows that men have changed, but not as much as women would have liked. So what does it mean to be a New New Man? Who is this guy?

The New New Man laughs out loud when he reads about 'manxiety' – the stress allegedly felt by the loss of male status in a world also allegedly dominated by women (where would that be exactly? The White House? Downing Street? The Kremlin?), and he wonders if men felt 'manxiety' when they were landing on the beaches of Normandy.

Yet the New New Man's life is not without hypertension – the pressure of earning a living while being a good father, a caring partner, an is-it-good-for-you-baby? lover.

The New New Man is pulled by the forces that have tormented women for decades – that constant striving not to have it all, but to do it all. And then get up the next day and do it all again.

The New New Man reacts to the demands on his time with an almost constant rage. Everything makes him angry, and yet he laughs a lot, and almost every word that comes out of his smirking mouth has a subtext of irony. He enjoys the company of men, and relaxes in their company, and opens up in a way that he rarely does with women.

The New New Man has noticed that there are now more women than men in employment, and this bothers him not a jot. He only cares about how well someone does their job. He has no interest in fumbles in the stationery cupboard – he is way too worldly for that. He knows that the problem in this world is not getting laid, but avoiding getting laid.

The New New Man is perhaps a better father than husband. He loves his children with a passion that frightens him. He feels guilty about them when he is not around.

The New New Man has no problem with a strict male grooming regime – he moisturises, when he remembers, though he can't be arsed to floss too often – but he knows that the way a man looks simply does not matter the way it does for women. He knows that rich, powerful men have never been lonely in all of human history, and that they never will be.

Above all, the New New Man does not feel remotely sorry for himself. He knows that being born a man is to get five balls in the lottery of life. Even now. He wouldn't swap.

The New New Man knows himself – he is aware that he has deep biological urges that have no place in a calm, quiet life, or our tame modern world. But he feels quite proud of the fact that more than anything he wants to be a good provider and protector of his family, not because he is the product of an oppressive, patriarchal society but because he loves them.

And despite what you may have heard, the New New Man has absolutely no problem with his partner bringing home the bacon. Just as long as she doesn't bring home more than him. That would be awful for the New New Man.

If you told him that masculinity was in crisis, he wouldn't agree. More than his father or grandfather, the New New Man feels free. He knows that he has never been tested – by war, by poverty, by a world without good coffee – the way that they were tested. But he also knows that in balancing all the elements of his life, from work to home and all stops in between, he is probably more of a man in full than Dad and Granddad ever were.

Read Germaine Greer's *The Female Eunuch* and you will see that the great visionary of feminism was not demanding a world where women were equal, but a world where women were free.

Free to fulfil their potential, free to be themselves. Isn't that exactly what the men of today want?

Free to be a man, my son.

Twenty-Three

Fever Bitch

I can't remember the day that I fell in love with football, but I can clearly remember the day I fell out of love.

It was a season not so long ago, when Arsenal were at Birmingham, the day that Eduardo almost had his foot torn from his leg.

It was one of those rare injuries that remind you that there is a world beyond the green green grass of home and away, a world where a word like 'tragedy' means something a bit more serious than a goal scored by the opposition in the final minute of extra time.

You might have thought that on such a day – when a young man was on his way to hospital not knowing if he would ever walk again, let alone play top-flight football – those who remained would have carried themselves with some dignity. But then along came Arsenal's alleged captain, William Gallas.

Birmingham were awarded a penalty right at the death, a chance to level a game where the result was meaningless judged next to Eduardo's injury, and Gallas – that doughty leader of men – flipped out. Total mental meltdown. Before Birmingham had even taken their penalty, Gallas had minced to the other end of the pitch where he bravely attacked an advertising hoarding. Then, after Birmingham had put away their penalty for a two-all draw, the Arsenal captain sat down on the pitch and burst into tears.

The thoughts of Tony Adams are unknown.

But in those few grotesque minutes, Gallas threw away Arsenal's season. They had not lost a match – although Eduardo had nearly lost a foot. They were still on course for the championship. And then along came Gallas and it was like seeing Churchill trying to surrender during the Battle of Britain. Morale collapsed.

It so happened that I was watching the match with a Junior Gunner who was wearing full replica kit – my then five-year-old daughter. Sulks, tantrums, girly fits – my daughter had never seen anything quite like William Gallas.

The *Daily Mirror* summed it up best – ARSENAL NEEDED TONY ADAMS AND THEY GOT BRITNEY SPEARS. And I knew that I just didn't care any more. It did not start with Gallas, but he shone a withering spotlight on my true feelings for the game that I had loved all my life.

And those true feelings were distaste, indifference and disgust.

When I was a boy one of my dreams was that I might see England win their second World Cup in my lifetime, but now

the very thought of even watching them makes my skin crawl
– all those flat-footed underachieving millionaires, all the thick
fans booing the opposition's national anthem, all the tiers of
empty seats after half-time because the boys in hospitality can't
tear themselves away from their prawn sandwiches. I haven't
been able to watch England for years, and now I find I can't
even follow my club.

And so it was that bleak mid-winter lashed at my window,
and then spring crept shyly in, and the FA Cup Final was played
– and I was shocked to realise that a season had come and
gone and, for the first year since I turned five, I had not been
to a single live match.

Gallas made me realise that I can't stand any of it any
more. Not the diving, not the cheating, not the falling over in
a strong breeze. There are still great players. Fàbregas, Torres,
Rooney – they would have graced the sport at any time in its
history. But the soul of football is now a rotting marshmallow.

Football was once a game played by men. And they were
hard men. I don't just mean the likes of Tony Adams and Roy
Keane, Tommy Smith and Billy Bremner, Dave MacKay and
Peter Storey. Even George Best, the most flamboyant footballer
that ever graced these islands, was made of Belfast steel. Same
with Rodney Marsh or Charlie George. They were Cavaliers
with the pain thresholds of Roundheads. Footballers today –
frankly, I've known harder hairdressers. Drogba, Eboué, Ronaldo
– these are big strong men who too often resemble Divine
Brown.

They just go down far too easily.

And don't get me started on the badge kissing. The likes of Ronaldo, Lampard and Adebayor (as the song says, give him eighty grand and he still wants more) spent one summer threatening to leave their clubs unless more money was found, and then they spent next season slobbering over their badges.

I wish I could just turn away from the whining, grasping players and the dumb, sheep-like fans and the diving, the cheating and the crybaby tears of William Gallas – but breaking with football is hard to do. Because there is always something there to remind me, and it is a lifetime of memories.

If I don't know exactly when I fell in love with football, then that is because football was always there. My mum had six brothers who supported West Ham and they were always happy to take me to watch Bobby Moore, Martin Peters, and Geoff Hurst – the West Ham team that won the World Cup.

I saw hundreds of games at Upton Park in those golden years and so I saw them all – the Chelsea of Peter Osgood, Ron Harris and Charlie Cooke, the Manchester United of Denis Law, Bobby Charlton and George Best, Don Revie's Leeds United, Bill Shankly's Liverpool, Bill Nicholson's Tottenham Hotspur.

Watching football in those days was rough, and those heaving, unregulated terraces and the streets and tube stations around the ground were often awash with violence. The worst

I ever saw was when Manchester United – immaculate in white shirts, white shorts and red socks – clinched a late-sixties league title at Upton Park with a 6–1 victory. Battles raged all afternoon as my uncles and I kept our heads down on a North Bank cranny known as The Shelf.

It was like being in the cheap seats at Agincourt.

Yet for generations of working-class men football was a reason to live. The toilets were rivers of piss. There were no women. Fans were treated like livestock. But for many of us, it was the closest we had ever come to a transcendent experience.

One of the great myths about football fans is that they are monogamous creatures who devote themselves to one club for a lifetime. This is not true, certainly not if you grow up in or around London. My mum's brothers, Fleet Street printers who didn't work on a Saturday, were all West Ham fans, but my dad was a Tottenham Hotspur fan. And although he was a greengrocer who had to work Saturdays, he would take me to White Hart Lane for mid-week games under the floodlights, and so away from Upton Park I had this other life watching Jimmy Greaves, Alan Gilzean and Cyril Knowles.

It was only when my uncles took me to watch West Ham play away against Arsenal at Highbury that I felt I had found a team of my own. I liked the Arsenal kit, the way the white sleeves looked against the red of the shirts, and I liked the stolidly English feel of Highbury – there was a brass band at half-time, a glimpse of marble halls, the bust of Herbert Chapman, powerful memories of England before the war. And I loved the floodlights, which ran around the roof of the ground in what looked like streams of white, pink and blue. The floodlights were better than the game.

There was a bit of an incident outside the ground. Ian Ure – Arsenal's big, blond Scottish centre half – had committed some offence against West Ham, and my uncles snarled and hissed at him in the street. Ure, dapper in a suit and club tie, just grinned. I was very impressed. West Ham were flamboyant, but Arsenal were hard. If West Ham and Arsenal had been ancient Greeks, then the Hammers would have been Athenians, and the Gunners Spartans.

Then I grew up, and I became a season ticket holder at Arsenal, and for twenty years I lived close enough to Highbury to walk to the ground. Then they moved and so did I. And while I could see that the Emirates was a far more beautiful stadium than Highbury, I just didn't like it as much. I loved the old English claustrophobia of Highbury, and the Art Deco stands, and the familiarity of something that remained largely unchanged in an ever-shifting world.

But football had been changing for years. And some of those changes were very necessary. The matches I attended as a child too often felt like riots at a Ku Klux Klan rally. The culture of violence that surrounded football led directly to fans being treated like cattle, and this dehumanisation in the name of crowd control led directly to the horrors of Hillsborough and Heysel.

Football changed because it could do nothing else. I remember going to half-empty grounds in the early eighties when it felt like any sane, civilised human being would be somewhere else. Anywhere else.

Then suddenly we had all-seater stadia, and segregated fans, and middle-class accents in the bar. You could buy a salmon bagel. Football was a safer, healthier, wealthier sport than the game I had known as a boy. You could even buy good books about football.

Then some unknown player fell over and howled in agony when he wasn't really hurt at all.

And something precious began to die.

For years and years, football was always there.

Bands would release a rubbish second album. Girls would pack you in. The drugs stopped working. But football never let you down, and even in those heaving grounds of the sixties and seventies where men relieved themselves in the pockets of other men, it was touched by a rough magic.

The feeling lasted for decades. Even when the game that I had grown up with was transformed by the Taylor report and the Premiership and an avalanche of TV money, it was still touched by magic. Because football had the endless ability to reinvent itself. Ian Wright was gone but along came Thierry Henry. Eric Cantona retired but there was still Beckham and then Ronaldo. And football could still produce a John Terry or

Wayne Rooney or Stephen Gerrard – skilled, hearts-of-oak Englishmen who would make the ghost of Bobby Moore smile with approval, footballers who would have graced the game before my voice changed.

But even as it produced all these new glories, and even as we sat wide-eyed in new stadiums, eating our salmon bagels, something was decomposing in the heart of the game. The dark side became part of the landscape.

The greed. The whining. The diving. The need to stuff your pockets and the impulse to win at all costs. I know that for every petulant Ashley Cole figure there is a Cesc Fàbregas or Fernando Torres. But the tone is set by the spoilt ones, the pampered ones, the scumbags. I can't jump to my feet and cheer them. I don't want to see Adebayor kiss his badge. I would need a big hole in the middle of my life to want to watch that.

Football is a game played by men and loved by boys. Even if the game had never changed, I could never love it quite as much as I did when I was fourteen. Something happens the moment you are older than the footballers. But I should still care. It should still matter. The love should be there.

Yet somewhere along the line, I started hating it. William Gallas did not make me fall out of love with football. The big French jessie just made me realise that the love had curdled to loathing.

And I find myself thinking of Arron and Ben Peak, two young brothers who were ten and eight when they died.

Luke McCormick, a twenty-five-year-old professional footballer, was twice the drink-driving limit and, the court was told, 'driving like an idiot', when he rammed his Range Rover into the back of a car carrying Arron, Ben and their father. The boys died. The father is now in a wheelchair with a damaged spine.

McCormick, a former Plymouth Argyle goalkeeper, was sent to jail but will be out before his thirtieth birthday. And, yes, I know that he is nobody. But I can't help but feel he embodies the rotten spirit of football today. Spoilt, selfish, stupid beyond belief.

And not worthy of the admiration of the boys he killed.

For in the smiling family photos of Arron and Ben Peak, the dead brothers hold their thumbs up and proudly wear the football shirts of their club and their country, Manchester United and England. Two little football fans who were killed by a drunken professional footballer who was upset about rumours on the Internet about his girlfriend.

And I wonder if the crippled father of those two young football fans watches *Match of the Day* from his wheelchair.

I find I don't bother any more.

Twenty-Four

Double Standards Now

Once upon a time double standards were heavily weighted in favour of men.

If a girl had meaningless sex with a string of anonymous strangers, then she was a filthy slag, a wanton strumpet, the Whore of Babylon.

But if a man had meaningless sex with a string of anonymous strangers, then he was Jack the Lad, the cock of the walk, Rod Stewart.

It was horribly unfair. And yet the injustice of it all did seem rooted in some inescapable biological fact. Namely, men need to spray their seed far and wide to ensure the survival of the species. Whereas women, by biological design, have to be infinitely more choosy. It takes nine months for a woman to make a baby and nine seconds for a man. Female eggs are more precious than those crafted by Fabergé. Sperm is cheap and plentiful.

But now the old double standards are being inverted. Men who get about a bit are no longer Rod Stewart. They are he-sluts.

When Mel Gibson pressed the 'eject' button on his wife Robyn and took up with a Russian minx called Oksana Grigorieva, women all over the world started spitting bile. Oh, how could he? For all his faults, Mel Gibson was one of the most emphatically married men in Hollywood – twenty-eight years and seven children with one woman. Much was made of Mel's physical decline from bright young thing to dirty old man. It was difficult to know what was harder for female critics to forgive – that Mel had taken up with a younger woman, or that he no longer looked like Mad Max. Barbara Ellen neatly captured the mood in *The Observer*.

'Do you like my bristly, grey-haired stomach rubbing against you like that?' she said, putting herself in Mel's orthopaedic shoes. 'Should I press harder with my man boobs? Is that really turning you on?'

What made the female outrage a little odd was that, when she hooked up with Menopausal Max, Oksana Grigorieva was approaching her fortieth birthday – hardly Lolita material.

'Young enough to be his daughter,' screeched many an anti-Mel blogger.

Well, just about. But Mel was only fourteen years old when Oksana was born.

After having a bit of fun with Mel's man boobs and sagging butt, and after a few taunts about his grey pubes and sagging beach shorts, Barbara Ellen gently pointed out the rank hypocrisy of women mocking old Mel for jumping on the bones of youngish Oksana. Because of course women do exactly the same thing – and get lavishly praised for it.

Thanks to the new double standards, when women take up with men who are many years their junior it is somehow symptomatic of their lust for life, their you-go-girl empowerment, their healthy Amazonian libido.

Demi Moore, forty-five, goes to sleep at night with hubby Ashton Kutcher, thirty-one, and it is called a May–December romance. Demi has become the Nelson Mandela of rumpy-pumpy – an inspiration to the enslaved women of the world. But Mel Gibson, fifty-three, lays down by the side of Oksana, thirty-nine, and he is a leper, a loser, worthy of nothing more than mocking laughter.

Spot the difference?

In terms of age there is none – Demi and Mel both having exactly fourteen years on their partners. But these days the sisters can get away with what the brothers simply cannot. It is naughty men who are the Whores of Babylon now.

Women can take up with younger guys and they are applauded, lauded and loved. They are even idealised. 'She understands how important it is to take control of her life,' gushed one American pundit of the older woman who likes younger men. 'She is a woman of style and grace. She is confident, beautiful, sexy and financially independent.'

Really? All of them? Honest? But nobody ever claimed that all men who court younger women look like George Clooney. They were always far more likely to look like Danny DeVito.

Ten years on from the birth of a Canadian website called cougardate.com, which promised to help older women find younger men, the cougar woman finally revealed her true nature when a fifty-three-year-old male movie star had the temerity to leave his wife for a woman who was cresting forty.

And now we know – the cougar woman is not really here to bonk you blind while her shagged-out ex-husband is at home with his lukewarm cocoa and his dying libido.

No – she exists to vividly demonstrate the new double standards and to reveal just how brutally the pendulum has swung in the other direction.

And smacked hard against our collective knackers.

Older women are a bit like policemen – you can never find one when you really need them.

I was twenty years old, my body tanned dark brown from the Mediterranean, penniless perhaps but in my sexual prime. And yet as I wandered the French Riviera all the length of that long, lost summer, it was clear that girls my own age were not looking for someone like me. They appeared to prefer men who had paunches and grey hair.

Oh yes – and boats.

They seemed quite fond of older men with boats – the bigger the boat, the more likely they were to overlook the physical imperfections that come to us all with time.

The Med of my youth was crawling with pot-bellied old men

surrounded by twenty-year-old beauties preening on the decks of their yachts. The image is burned on my memory like the tattoo on a lap dancer's arse. It will never go away. *This is how the world is,* I thought. *Get used to it.*

While the old men entertained the young women on their boats, I kipped down in my lonely sleeping bag on the beach, their laughter drifting across to me as I cried myself to sleep. One morning I awoke with the toe of a gendarme's boot up my bottom. It was the closest I came all summer to any kind of sexual experience.

There was no army of cougar women to salve my loneliness. There were no confident, beautiful, sexy older women to share my pain. Actually, there was one. She was a Med-dwelling Brit who was around forty, and my youthful budgie-smugglers caught her eye. I went to her room. She closed the door. She sat on the bed with one of those silky, floaty things above her bikini. We talked. And it might have happened. But it didn't. Because her ex-husband was flying down to visit their teenage daughter the next day, and she did not want him to see her with a twenty-year-old hitchhiker. For being with me and my budgie-smugglers would not have shown her ex-husband how far she had come, but how low she had sunk.

How times have changed. And only for the better. Nobody has to be alone in their sleeping bag any more. The mutton shall lay down with the lamb – whatever your gender.

I am all in favour of older women netting younger men – and I would be even more in favour of them if I was still twenty years old. But is preferring your fruit when it is a bit on the green side really a philosophy for life? Or is it just a sexual preference?

There have always been older women. It wasn't a creed. It wasn't a seismic social shift. It wasn't like now. Often, your encounter with an older woman was a one-off, a beautiful aberration. Usually, they were not even old – late twenties, early thirties at most. It was all relative. And I don't mean that she was your auntie.

And older women – really older women – have never looked better than they do today. Changed attitudes to exercise, diet and dentistry mean that there is now a generation of fifty-something women who could make a dead man come. Often they look infinitely hotter than women who could be their children. Give me Marie Helvin (fifty-six), Sharon Stone (fifty-one) and Kim Basinger (fifty-five) over Britney Spears (twenty-eight), Lindsay Lohan (twenty-two) or Peaches Geldof (twenty) any day of the year.

But the older woman looking for a lad in Diesel jeans is no more likely to resemble Sharon Stone than an old bull is prone to look like Hugh Grant (fifty in 2010). 'I would rather date a sexy hunk than a flabby chunk,' says Cher.

Yes, but wouldn't we all, dear?

The gaggle of forty-something women recently wheeled out to state the cougar case to Middle England in the *Daily Mail*, were – with the best will in the world – more flabby chunk than sexy hunk. But then the new double standards are blind.

Their rhetoric was full of young investment bankers gagging for older women in King's Road bars, but the accompanying pictures were of three heavy, rather desperate-looking women. They admired Joan Collins but they were built like Johnny Vegas.

But that information is suppressed. You can mock Mel Gibson's 'man boobs' all you like, but don't you dare notice anything starting to sag or crack on, say, Madonna. The harsh truth is that these self-professed cougar women often look as ropey as any dirty old goat with a well-worn medallion.

Valerie Gibson doesn't tell you that in her seminal book, *Cougar – A Guide for Older Women Dating Younger Men*. And they don't tell you that in the Faye Dunaway movie *Cougar Club*. And they don't tell you about the ropey factor on sites like www.dateacougar.com. Why would they?

God knows the younger men they 'date' look even ropier. The new double standards censor the information that these younger men are mostly bottom feeders preying on vulnerable, usually divorced women. Of course they go out with women old enough to be their mothers.

What women their own age would want them?

The fact is that older women date younger men for exactly the same reasons that older men date younger women.

Firm, springy bodies. A lack of bitterness. A lack of disappointment. A lack of moping teenage children cluttering up the house. Time to waste. The possibility of having beautiful babies.

And, most of all, because they can.

Whether you are looking for a lifelong commitment or a mini-break, you probably have more chance of making it go with a bang with a lover who is a bit younger than you are. Earthlings become harder work as they get older. So let ye who is without sin cast the first stone at Mel Gibson's man boobs.

Men can hardly complain that women are starting to do what we have done throughout history. We can all understand why a man or woman with a few miles on the clock would want to jump on the bones of someone in their physical prime. On a biological level, nothing could be more natural, or make more perfect sense. And in a recession, there is always room for May–December romances, where one side has the youth and beauty while the other side has the money and the titanium AmEx card.

The boys of our time have no jobs, no money, and they will have to live at home with their parents until they are forty-nine. Traditionally, the meeting of sex and economics has always been the older man with the younger woman, but there is nothing in the rulebook to say that it can't work the other way round.

What I can't get my head around – because I am still acclimatising to the new double standards – is why mixed-age dating is inherently noble when women do it.

And inherently nasty when men do it.

'Don't ever let age stop you from getting what you want,' says one cougar woman blogger. 'Age is just a number. Attract what you want by being what you want. Embrace happiness. Don't be guided by fear. Don't hand over your sexuality or sensuality with your fortieth or fiftieth birthday. You deserve it all!'

True enough!

And I know you will not mind if I say exactly the same thing to Peter Stringfellow.

Twenty-Five

Fake Breasts Don't Bounce Back

In the war against fake breasts, we may have reached the Normandy landings.

I say to you all today that this is not the end of fake breasts. This is not even the beginning of the end of fake breasts. But it is, perhaps, the end of the beginning.

Her nipples proudly pointing the way forward to a better, bouncier, happier, healthier tomorrow, Victoria Beckham has chosen to reduce her surgically enhanced – pause to vomit balls out of mouth at loathed infantile euphemism – 'boobs'.

According to the *Sunday Mirror*'s breast correspondent, Victoria's recent downsizing is her third procedure. The paper reports that the first was in 1999 when Posh had her pert, perfectly lovely, God-given 34A breasts increased to an eye-watering, gawd-blimey-you-don't-get-many-of-those-to-the-pound-guvnor 34DD.

Now she has gone from those Jessica Rabbit-sized 34DDs to an infinitely more modest 34B, which do not draw quite so much attention to themselves at the school gates – or at least no longer stand up and wave hello to the other parents.

So after all that surgery, Mrs Beckham is practically back to where she started.

And for those of us who are resolute in our opposition to the female mutilation that we euphemistically call 'fake boobs', it feels like the landing craft have just hit the beach.

Fake breasts are still out there. Fake breasts remain a growth industry. Fake breasts still abound.

Among celebrities, among 'ordinary' people. Among all sorts of thickos, rich and poor and everywhere in between who have absolutely no idea of the risks and the ruin they are imposing upon themselves by buying their breasts off the shelf.

Boobs?

You said it.

Those of us who have some inkling of the horror of fake breasts should not get too excited. The war is not yet won. The Red Army are not yet smashing their way into Berlin.

The media were recently beating a path to the door of the most surgically enhanced family in the country – the Marshalls of Kirkby-in-Ashfield, a mother and four daughters who have spent £40,000 on nine breast operations. One paper gasped, 'That makes them the British family who have had the most breast surgery – BRA none!'

Geddit? Bra none! I geddit, I geddit!

It would be tempting to say that the stupid will always be with us. But it is not just thickness that propels a woman and her shockingly young daughters into mutilating themselves. It is a heartbreaking combination of insecurity, unhappiness and the delusion that breasts are like those rubber meals you see in the windows of restaurants in Japan – there to be looked at, and nothing more.

Mum-of-nine Chantal confessed, 'Having nine children left my boobs looking like milk bottles. In 1996, after I had my seventh child, I had my first set of implants but I ended up even unhappier. They looked like balls in socks rather than the pert, round breasts I had imagined. I was quite traumatised.'

Chantal's surgically enlarged daughters – the youngest just eighteen – encouraged their dear old mum to go back on the butcher's slab. Chantal now displays her 32GG breasts as proudly as if they were an Open University degree.

At the celebrity end of the market, you still see poor deluded souls like *Coronation Street* star Kym Marsh displaying her new breasts as though they are something she has just won in a raffle – or as if they could possibly be any kind of improvement on what she had before.

Yet the trend is definitely and overwhelmingly away from doing a Jordan. In fact, it is grossly unfair to Katie Price/Jordan to portray her as the patron saint of artificial breasts. The glamour girl has gone from 32FF to 32D – her fourth procedure and first reduction.

In the current less-is-much-more climate, not even Jordan is doing a Jordan.

Ulrika Jonsson saw her cup size soar to 34I – roughly the diameter of downtown Malmo – while breastfeeding her youngest child. She slimmed down naturally to 32E and then had breast reduction to bring her down to 32C. Shy, retiring Kerry Katona was seen on MTV having a breast-reduction op that took her from 34GG to 34DD.

'They have just got a bit out of control,' said Kerry, as though her breasts had a wild social life of their own. Kimberly Stewart and Denise Richards have also ditched the silicone. Why is the tide turning?

Because implants make real breasts feel lifeless? Because a woman who has had a breast operation will often discover that she no longer has a matching pair? Because fake 'boobs' make breast cancer, lumps and tumours infinitely harder to detect? Because fakes cause endless pain, suffering and loss of sensitivity?

Or is it just because Victoria Beckham thinks fake breasts are so over?

Possibly.

Fake breasts have been sold as a style statement, rather than voluntary disfigurement, as something akin to a fake tan rather than an act of female mutilation to rival anything they get up to in the Third World.

Poor, ignorant people inflict clitoridectomies and try to render the practice harmless by calling it female circumcision.

Rich, ignorant people call breast mutilation 'boob jobs'.

It's all surgery as human vandalism – about as healthy and necessary as the late Michael Jackson's removable nose.

The crucial difference between female circumcision and a 'boob job' is that no female in sub-Saharan Africa does it of her own free will.

It could be that the reasons fake breasts have finally fallen out of favour are as trivial as the reasons they were once all the rage.

Victoria Beckham's official spokesperson declined to take the media on a voyage around her client's breasts – funny that – but a source told the *Sun*, 'Victoria has wanted her implants taken out for a while. She felt that was part of the old WAG image – the big hair, big boobs and fake tan – and that she has moved on since those days. She is very pleased with the results. After the operation she came to London for business and then went to France to heal properly in private.'

But even if they are only edging away from fake breasts because of fashion, women are at last waking up to something that men have known since they first laid their trembling hands on stiff, unyielding breasts containing silicone implants.

Real ones are always, always better.

Fake breasts are a bucket of cold water chucked on male desire.

Leaving aside all the medical arguments against saline-filled

and silicone-gel-filled implants – and those arguments should
be enough – they just don't feel good.

They are hard. Unmoving. Unreal.

This is what heterosexual women have never, and could
never understand – what it feels like to touch fake breasts in
the heat of passion.

For years the overwhelming majority of men have been
telling pollsters that, in the words of one survey of nearly two
thousand eighteen- to thirty-four-year-old men, *'Boob jobs are
a complete turn-off.'*

Then how to explain the popularity of Jordan before her
sudden enlightenment? And how to explain the popularity of
glamour girls and porn stars, whose fake breasts are as manda-
tory as the teeth-whitening and old Tango tans?

Ah, but it's not those breasts that matter, it's what they
represent. Fake breasts convey a message of easy virtue,
sexual licence, half a shandy and she's anybody's. Fake
breasts have a sky-high Slut Factor, and that will always have
crowd appeal.

Little boys – and overgrown boys – adore fakes. The kind
of grubby little boys who lock themselves in the bathroom and
then tremble at every creak on the staircase.

'What are you doing in there?'

'Nothing, Mum.'

But we know, don't we?

The overwhelming majority of men hate fake breasts. Boys

like them, because they do not know what a real breast actually feels like.

Or a real lady.

The best argument I ever heard in favour of fakes was when I was on the *Richard and Judy Show* with Jodie Marsh, taking part in the great national boob debate.

Another guest, a woman still in possession of her own natural breasts, said that she was divorced, in her forties, and when she went out with a new man, if they ended up having sex then he would be seeing her for the very first time as a middle-aged mother. She was self-conscious about what he might think – and that was why she was tempted to climb on to the surgeon's slab.

And anyone can understand that argument.

If you stay with one woman for years, then it seems natural to watch their body change – as the years roll by, as the children come along.

But in a culture where everyone is always starting over, you always want to look your best – even if your best was twenty years ago. Yet fake breasts are never the answer.

Those hard, unmoving, unlovable monstrosities can never be an improvement on reality. I can see how, on a night of moonlight and Pinot Noir, a surgically enhanced silhouette might momentarily capture the imagination. But in the morning you would both still be waking up with a pair of store-bought breasts between you.

And as for Jodie Marsh, she was a nice enough girl. She said that she agreed with many of the anti-fake arguments but she was in a glamour profession, competing for the attention of the photographers with girls ten years her junior. When we went to a commercial break, I asked her what her boyfriend thought of her body.

'I don't have a boyfriend,' she said.

I don't know if I could ever love a woman with fake breasts. That's how superficial I am.

I know from my years as a single guy that I could have sex with her. But I don't know if I could ever really love her. And it wouldn't be the kind of sex that you would want to repeat until the end of days. It would be more like the kind of sex you do for half a drunken hour, and then can't remember.

Because beyond the health factor, and beyond the aesthetics, there's a banality about fake breasts. It's like when you see someone with a big tattoo – it's like announcing, 'I have an MBA in being a moron.' And there is a conceit about fake breasts. Look at me, they squeak, even as they are lying there as lifeless as a pair of dead tuna.

Does Victoria Beckham regret ever going under the surgeon's knife? She doesn't talk about it, so we will never know. But after becoming a mother, her natural 34A breasts would have grown anyway. That's what women do – they change.

And if you are a man, and if you have two brain cells to rub together, and if you love this person, then you embrace that change. Most women get sexier as they get older. If nothing ever changed, there would be no butterflies.

And I shall always ponder this great central mystery about unnecessary breast surgery. During the long years of fake-boob fever, where were the female voices of protest?

Why weren't intelligent women marching in the street protesting this mammary madness? Where were the feminists?

How could thinking women ever allow unthinking women to believe that getting breast implants was as harmless as getting highlights?

As the father of a daughter, I object to the way that breast surgery is even now presented by our dumb society as something trivial rather than an act of self-mutilation. I have heard the latest Posh procedure described as having 'a little off the top'.

A little off the top?

That is what you have at the barber's.

Not on the surgeon's slab.

Twenty-Six

The Secret of My Failure

The secret of my failure was that I thought success was permanent.

Like a lot of men, I had reached a sweet-scented peak that I thought was mine for life. And then one foul day I fell into the pit of failure. And then came, oh, ten years where the postman became the most important person in my diminished life, because his footsteps outside our shabby little flat brought the possibility of some paltry cheque.

Ten years of fretting about money. Ten years of waking up in the middle of the night wondering where the next mortgage payment was coming from. Ten years to contemplate where it had all gone wrong. And ten years of dreading that inevitable moment at a party when someone asked, 'And what are *you* doing these days?'

The funny thing is, I was working like a dog. Taking any job that came my way because failures can't be choosers. But it didn't make any difference. All successful men work hard, but so do the vast majority of unsuccessful men. Funny that.

I had left my first job in journalism, as a staff writer on *NME*, with great expectations. I was twenty-five years old and for the last three years I had been writing stories for the biggest music weekly in the world. I was quite popular, I thought – but it was only when I left the *NME* that I discovered I was only popular with nineteen-year-old high-IQ misfits who were saving up for their first pair of bondage trousers. Nobody else had heard of me. Nobody else wanted to know.

And in rapid succession I was married, a father, divorced and a single father. I wanted to work. But there was not enough work. And even when there was work, they took their time paying me. For a single man, failure is hard to take. For a family man, especially a broken family man, it is poison. This went on for most of the eighties. No red braces for me. No greed-is-good. No flutes of champagne under a Thatcherite sky. This was the other eighties, where your youth got buried under all those red bills.

Here is how failure finds you. First there is a creeping sense of dread and then suddenly the roof caves in.

'How did you go bankrupt?' asks a character in *The Sun Also Rises.*

'Two ways,' comes the reply. 'Gradually and then suddenly.'

That is how failure hits you.

Gradually and then suddenly.

Slowly, almost imperceptibly at first – the increasing struggles with money, the nagging sense of things not going how you had expected, how you would like, and then the terrible

realisation that the world can get along without you just fine –
and finally disaster. The bills that can't be paid. The career in
the ditch. The relationship in ruins. Your health shot.

Jay McInerney uses that quote from Hemingway's novel at
the start of his own masterpiece, *Bright Lights, Big City*. One
of the ultimate zeitgeisty eighties books, *Bright Lights, Big City*
is really the story of a young man failing – chemically, professionally, economically, personally, socially. All the ways we can
fail.

For all its references to Bolivian Marching Powder and clubs
and girls with shaven heads, *Bright Lights, Big City* is really the
best novel ever written about coping with failure, and taking
the first tentative steps to recovery.

McInerney's novel ends with the protagonist trading his
sunglasses for some freshly baked bread, down on his knees,
stuffing it into his mouth, and trying to keep it down.

That's what fighting failure feels like. It turns your stomach.
It feels like it might just be beyond you.

I felt that way for ten years. From the middle of my twenties until the middle of my thirties, I was that man on his knees,
struggling to keep the fresh bread in his stomach.

And there was no great shining moment when I felt failure
was behind me. After ten years of hard slog, holding on, getting
by, and sometimes not quite getting by, things started to turn
the corner.

There was money, there was opportunity, there was the
ebbing away of anxiety. But when you have known failure – real,

kick-in-the-bollocks failure – it never really leaves you, and you take nothing for granted.

Things change. The new boss doesn't like you as much as the old boss. There are tensions in the office. You are overlooked for a promotion/raise/blow-job at the office party. You get sacked. Or you feel hemmed in, unfulfilled and frustrated. You move on. And stumble. And fall. And fail.

Every heroic myth has failure built into the narrative. We think of Ali with his jaw broken in the first fight against Joe Frazier, Sinatra in the dog days with no recording contract, Christ on the cross in his moment of doubt and pain. But we all know how the story ends – that Ali will meet Frazier again in Manila, and that Sinatra has Capitol Records and *From Here to Eternity* around the corner, and on the third day the stone will roll back and eternal life awaits.

Great men overcome failure and it makes them greater than ever. But when you can't pay your gas bill you don't feel like Muhammad Ali or Frank Sinatra or Jesus Christ. You feel more like Mr Bean.

They say that failure isn't fatal. But it doesn't feel that way when you are in the middle of it. Failure feels like it will kill you. Failure is the dirty bomb in the life of the modern male, as undeniable as serious illness, a condition it closely resembles.

Looking on the bright side, my decade of failure didn't kill me. Somehow the bills got paid. I never went bankrupt. Although what happened to me was personally devastating, and not what I would have wanted, some people might even consider it a kind of measly, modest success. I never had a boss, or had to go to an office, or had to wear a suit and tie when I didn't want to. I kept working at the job I love – just about. I held on by the skin of my chewed fingernails. One man's abject failure is another man's bad decade at the office. Failure is relative.

At the start of *Broadcast News*, the Albert Brooks character is seen being given a beating as a swotty little schoolboy who is despised by the jocks.

'Go ahead,' he tells his tormentors, as they flatten his nose. 'But what I am going to say can never be erased. It will scar you forever. Ready? Here it is – you will never make more than nineteen thousand dollars a year! Ha ha ha!'

'Nineteen thousand dollars?' one of the bullies says thoughtfully. 'Not bad . . .'

There are a thousand ways for a man to feel like a failure but nothing cuts to the bone quite as acutely as professional failure because so much of male self-esteem is derived from what we do for a living.

So how to fight failure? Stay fit. Work hard. Then work harder. Then work better. No drinking to excess over the age of thirty. No drugs at all over the age of twenty-five. Never let your vices become your day job. Never get lazy. Never get fat. And never *ever* bet against yourself.

There is no shame in failing. Great men have spent a lifetime on their knees. In his middle twenties, Orson Welles was cinema's favourite son. Then came decades of development hell. 'Something always turns up when you are down and out,' said Welles. 'Usually the noses of your friends.'

By the end, the man who had made *Citizen Kane* was making sherry commercials. But a failure? I don't think so.

'Sometimes a man can be destroyed but not defeated,' said Hemingway, who changed American literature but ended up one sunny Sunday morning, aged sixty-one, with his favourite double-barrelled 12-bore Boss shotgun pressed against the roof of his mouth. They say that his wife Mary was woken by two shots that were almost, but not quite, simultaneous. But a failure? As time goes by, Hemingway's life seems more like a triumph, even though the colossus was torn down at the end by the nightmare-ticket failure of body and mind.

Hemingway believed that any story, followed to the very end, would be a story of failure, and perhaps that is how we need to think of it. Failure – financial, professional, personal – is not a cruel act of God but an inevitable fluctuation in life's fortunes. You *will* get sacked. You *will* get sick. You *will* run out of money and time and luck. You *will* get your heart pulped by your true love. Failure in one shape or another will get you because it gets all of us sooner or later.

Failure hardens you. This is a good thing. You get sacked and you find out who your friends are. You get your heart broken and you learn that you give it away too easily. You get sick and you realise that you took your healthy flesh and blood for granted in your carefree, drug-sozzled youth.

The big problem with failure is that it is so time-consuming.

When you are worried about money, your mind has no room for anything else. When the red bills are on your doormat you find it hard to lift your eyes to the stars. But failure is the best education that money can't buy. It will ultimately do you a lot more good than going to 'uni' for three years.

Perhaps real and lasting success is impossible without the experience of real, grown-up failure. Until you have lost that job and lost that woman and watched your self-esteem running down the drain, you will never truly have lift-off.

In the School of Hard Knocks, genuine grinding failure – the kind where people wonder whatever happened to you, *and so do you* – is like a Double First from Oxford.

Surviving failure makes you a man. It makes you run twice as fast as the competition, it makes you twice as hungry, it makes you twice as hard. Once you have had your nose rubbed in the dirt – when you have spent hours beyond counting, just waiting for the postman to bring some dinky cheque – then the competition has no chance. The safe little flight plans of your rival's life – from school to university to office – are no match for what you have endured.

When it is happening to you, failure feels like a beating. It literally feels like you are on the sharp end of a kicking. And as anyone who has taken a good hiding will tell you, it is not the pain that hurts. It is the humiliation. Failure is like that. You taste it in the back of your throat.

But it puts some steel in your spine. It leaves a chip of ice in your heart. It makes you ready for anything. You always remember what failure felt like. And you remember it every day of your working life.

How dumb was I in my twenties? This dumb – when failure came looking for me, I was shocked. When I lost the job – when the money ran out – when serious illness found my family – when I was wearing my Harrington jacket to a divorce court – I was stunned that any of this could happen to me.

'Nothing bad ever happened to me before,' I said to my mother, as though that meant nothing bad *could* ever happen to me. That's why it took me ten long years to climb back. I didn't see failure coming. And I honestly thought it never would.

Don't be like me. Bounce back fast. Expect failure to hit you hard somewhere along the line. But I promise you this – if you lose the job, then you will find a better job. And if you lose the girl, then you will find a better girl. And if you lose your health, then you will cherish your health.

Embrace failure. Make it your greatest ally.

Because at the very moment they all think you are finished, and they are all betting against you, your success is assured.

Twenty-Seven

Why Men Stray,
Why Men Stay

At ten years old he wants to be tough.

At twenty he wants to be cool.

At thirty he wants to be free.

At forty he wants to belong.

At fifty he wants to be fit.

At sixty he wants to be rich.

At seventy he wants to be healthy.

At eighty he wants to be alive.

The difficult bit is accommodating the wish to be free and the need to belong.

The difficult bit has always been balancing the yearning for an impressive sexual CV and the longing for a wife, family, and home.

The need to be free and the need for home. Age has something to do with what men want – the younger man is more likely to see the attraction of multiple partners, while the older man will agonise if he has brought no children into the world.

But age is not everything.

Even this late in the day, there are plenty of men – especially among the working and upper classes – who get married and start having children in their twenties. And of course the swinging forty-something, fresh from the divorce court and ready to have another crack at the old dating game, is always with us.

Some men stay early.

Some men stray late.

Age is much less important than the two impulses. And men spend a lifetime trying to negotiate a peace settlement between these two most basic of instincts.

Men want to stay.

And men want to stray.

How can they want both?

Understand that, and you unlock the mystery of male behaviour.

Not all men stray. And some men stray for a bit and then they settle down. That is what many women find difficult to accept – that sometimes a man strays not because he is a heartless, fornicating bastard, but simply because he has not yet met the right girl.

As a general rule, poor men stray because of opportunity (Mavis in the stationery cupboard), and rich men stray because of a sense of entitlement (VIP areas stuffed with willing lovelies).

When Tiger Woods made his public confession after his tsunami of shagging became public knowledge, he was criticised for apologising to his corporate sponsors as well as his wife. And yet in those thirteen minutes of confession, Tiger Woods perfectly summed up why the billionaire Alpha Male can love his wife and children, and yet also love having sex with porn stars.

Look beyond that sterile, stage-managed setting, and you had Tiger Woods giving what was practically the Gettysburg Address of Infidelity.

'I thought I could get away with whatever I wanted to,' said a dazed-looking Tiger. 'I felt I had worked hard and deserved to enjoy all the temptations around me. I felt I was entitled.'

He felt that he was entitled. Simple as that. Lives turned inside out, oceans of hurt and betrayal to last a lifetime, pain to carry with you to the grave – and all because Tiger felt that he was well within his rights to do exactly what he wanted. He summed it up perfectly.

No group of thick Premiership footballers, roasting some poor slapper in their post-match hotel room, could explain their behaviour with such devastating psychological honesty. Because they are too stupid. But Tiger Woods did it – *I do these things because I have earned them*.

What is most interesting about Tiger Woods – and all the pea-brained Premiership footballers with all their hard-faced glamour girls – is not that they have a bit on the side. Men are hard-wired to spread those little wiggly things far and wide, and the constraints that rein in most men – social, economic, having to do the school run or get up for work in the morning – and loving someone – simply do not apply to the medium-sized swinging dicks of professional sport. They are not frightened of their wives. Only the wrath of the media keeps them in line.

No, the wonder is not that they stray. The wonder is that they almost always have a beautiful wife and lovely children back at home.

Think about it – the world is your knocking shop. Women are everywhere. Yet – even if you play for Chelsea – you still want to meet that special girl, and win her heart, and get married and have kids. Why bother? Why not just stay single?

Because the impulse to stay is at least as strong as the impulse to stray. *At least.*

The great irony is that men – rich men, poor men, and every economic bracket in between – risk everything for sex that is probably nowhere near as good as what they can get at home, and definitely with a woman who is not even remotely playing in the same league as their wife.

Consider the pictures of Tiger's harem – that motley, plain-faced crew of cocktail waitresses, porn stars and single soccer moms. What man in his right mind would trade the lot of them for Elin, the Swedish angel who married Tiger, and gave him his children?

Commenting on how he remained faithful to his wife when surrounded by the kind of Tinsel Town temptations that today's fornicating sportsmen could hardly imagine, Paul Newman famously said, 'You don't go out for hamburger when you have steak at home.'

But men do.

Oh yes, Paul – men go out for a Big Mac when they have prime fillet waiting at home. Men go out for fish fingers when sushi is in the fridge. Men go out for KFC nuggets when they have prime leg and breast at home. It is a kind of insanity, and the only possible explanation is that the male mind craves a varied diet. It does not mean he actually prefers hamburger.

Yet, incredibly, men are more than mindless sperm-making machines. And we want more than a lifetime of musical beds. Any man that has had periods of extreme promiscuity knows that it palls. In fact, it's often the men who have lost count who are the keenest to settle down.

When I was a lad on the *NME*, I knew a British musician who toured America and had a girl waiting for him in every hotel lobby in every city. These jaw-dropping drawer-dropping beauties in skin-tight leather trousers. I remember one in Philadelphia who had a suitcase full of whips, paddles and furry handcuffs. I had never seen anything like it in Billericay.

The world was post-Pill and pre-AIDS – the high tea of sexual liberation. And yet that musician – the one with the whip-lady in Philadelphia waiting for him – was one of the very first to find a pretty girl, and marry her, and have children that he adored.

That is men for you. Secretly, we want a family as much as any woman. We want the whole package – a loving wife, bright-eyed children, and a home. We want to belong. We *really* want to belong. And we want it at least as much as we want to spray our seed in the hotel rooms of the Eastern seaboard.

Belonging – we can want it too much. Those of us who were raised in nuclear families grew up thinking that making a home was easy. And those who were raised in families with divorced parents often feel compelled to try to restore that broken home.

Either way, men are like Bridget Jones after half a bottle of Chardonnay with 'All By Myself' on the Bose – full of dopey dreams, and unrealistic expectations, and doomed fantasies. And desperation – that's what men really share with Bridget Jones. That desperation to meet and marry Miss Right – especially after a few dozen brief encounters with Miss Right This Very Minute.

For the next generation of young men, it will become harder to stay and easier to stray.

In the old days, we learned our hard lessons about the opposite sex from real girls and real women.

Now that pornography is just another utility, as freely available as electricity and water, many men are being warped by the propaganda of hard core. And a man will never be capable of staying long when the majority of his memorable sexual encounters happened with his MasterCard in one hand and his mouse in the other.

We could save ourselves – and our girlfriends and our wives – so much trouble if we could have a period of wanton straying, followed by decades of blissful staying. What a wonderful world it could be. But it doesn't work that way.

Our twin basic instincts must forever live together in uneasy peace, punctuated by periods of bloody conflict. The need to stray and the need to stay – it is the Middle East of the male soul.

The good news is that it doesn't go on forever. In the life of most men, there is a final battle between straying and staying. You do – if you are wise, if you are lucky – get to that Paul Newman moment when you say – You know what? I am really sick of bloody fish fingers.

We want it so bad.

But to make it work – to reach Paul Newman Valhalla – you need to have had your fill of hamburger. There can be no staying without the straying. The tragedy is that sometimes men get it all the wrong way round. They do their staying. And then they really get stuck into their straying.

It's easy to get your timing all wrong. I was married in my mid-twenties – a traditional wedding with a pregnant bride – and it came apart before I was thirty. Then I was single for most of my thirties, going through a period of promiscuity when I slept with – for example – my neighbour, my neighbour's au pair and my neighbour's hamster.

Or did I just imagine the hamster?

But I was off the rails. Then I met my wife. And then I got married and became a dad again. And it was all saner, happier, better. Much better.

And there have been times when I thought that nobody could get their staying and their straying timing as badly wrong as me. But I do not feel that way any more. Because of my children. If the timing had been different, then those children would never have been born.

And I liked being a young dad in my twenties. As my friends grovelled in the sands of Ibiza beaches, off their faces on Ecstasy, I was reading *Where the Wild Things Are* to my little boy. Everything was against being a father that young – money, love, common sense.

Everything was against it. Apart from nature.

Nature wasn't against me being a dad in my twenties. Nature was all for it.

And so it felt right, being a father in my twenties. It felt like this was what I was on Earth to do.

Yet there is no denying that there were ten years of straying still on my to-do list. There is no denying that teardrops would fall because I stayed, then strayed and had to stray before I could stay again, and stay forever.

That's the way we are – programmed to pine for a family of our own, yet biologically bound to wander. Rich men are no different to other men – they just have increased opportunities.

'I was surprised to find that Tiger Woods was the unfaithful type,' said psychologist Oliver James.

But Tiger is sport's first self-made billionaire – how could he possibly be anything other than torn by the longing to stay, and the longing to stray? Tiger's beautiful wife is as inevitable as Tiger's mistresses. If Tiger just wanted to be a knob merchant, he could have stayed single. But the need for a loving family was as strong in him as the need for sex with the star of *Diary of a Horny Housewife.*

The staying should never be second best. The staying should matter more than the straying. The staying is what the straying should lead to. Look at Warren Beatty. Warren is not going out on the pull tonight. Because once you have had enough sex, the staying is better than the straying.

How can we want both? What cackling God made us want to stay and want to stray?

Because the secret of life is more life.

It is true, you know. At thirty a man wants to be free. He really does.

But in some secret chamber of his heart, he always wants to belong.

Twenty-Eight

The Formerly Young

'All children, except one, grow up.'

But J.M. Barrie, the creator of Peter Pan, did not live long enough to see middle-aged men in replica football shirts, or grey-haired groovers doing Class-A powders and Class-B puff at the weekend as though the sun never went down on Ibiza. Barrie never saw the slapheads, wrinklies and crinklies of every description listening to – and trying to love! – and actually downloading! – new music even when the new music has become hard work.

Barrie was spared the sorry sight of the generations who have found growing up impossible.

It's not just Peter Pan these days.

It is all of us.

Despite our glorious youth, we are no longer the young. And despite clinging to the detritus of youth – the unlovable new music, the Jeremy Clarkson denim, the pretend football shirts – we can't call ourselves old.

We are the formerly young.

*   *   *

Nobody gets old any more. Not the way our fathers and grandfathers got old. Not the way nature built us to grow old.

We stay forever formerly young.

You keep that Liam Gallagher haircut even when the thatch is grey and thinning. You wear that replica football shirt even though you are far too old to even be a referee in the Premiership. And you listen to new music even though in your heart you know – you *know* – that there hasn't been a truly great British band since the Stone Roses.

It's official – you are one of the formerly young.

Vanity Fair recently tried to explain Lady Gaga to its formerly young readers.

'A helpful decoding of the new pop landscape for the no longer hip,' was the promise. And I thought – Does anyone really want to try that hard to keep a finger on pop's dying pulse?

To which the formerly young cry – Hell, yeah!

Vanity Fair informed the formerly young that Lady Gaga equals Grace Jones minus Nona Hendryx divided by Peggy Lee plus 0.25 Freddie Mercury. And there was me thinking that Lady Gaga was simply a pre-menopause Madonna.

And as 'I Like It Rough' blared from my weary speakers, I asked myself – Is it worth the effort? And who cares? Ironically, only the people who would have once known instinctively what music meant, and exactly what it was worth, but who now need a diagram.

The formerly young need to know.

The whole drugs thing was over by the time he was twenty-five.

Goodbye and good riddance, he thought. Oh, there had been some fun along the chemical autobahn, but in the end there was only sadness, exhaustion and lives that resembled car wrecks.

By twenty-five, he was glad to get out more or less intact. The drugs got old.

Still, when some nice white-collar professional with a gram inside his pin-stripe suit offered him a line ten years later, well, he found that he just couldn't say no.

Why not? He knew he was electing to turn into a dead end. Was he afraid of being rude? Was he nostalgic for the days when he stayed up until dawn, setting the world to rights, talking rubbish and grinding his teeth? Was he afraid of missing out on the party or of spoiling it for others?

No – he did those little white lines so late in the day simply because he was afraid that abstaining would mean he was no longer young, no longer fun, no longer as in touch with the life force as he used to be. But that unwanted cocaine didn't prove that he was not yet old. They only proved that he was now formerly young.

Cocaine in his thirties – what was he thinking of? Was he to be stuck for the rest of his life in the twilight zone between youth and maturity? Would he always reject the chance to grow old gracefully?

When he knew he should aspire to becoming David Attenborough, would he always settle for being Ronnie Wood?

Must he stay forever formerly young?

In some parts of the world, old age is a licence to act badly. Or at least, to be forever pulling rank. In Japan and China, for example, it is quite common for old geezers to scream and shout and offer unsolicited advice at the top of their ancient voices.

I have been on a railway platform in Tokyo, and had some old fellow shouting that my daughter was too near the edge of the platform. Over here, of course, we would sling the interfering old git on the railway tracks. Over there, you are obliged to listen.

In Asia, old age means wisdom, experience, knowledge. Old age means that you have been on this crazy trip for quite a while and have learned a thing or two. As the French thinker Joseph Joubert said, 'Life is a country that the old have seen, and lived in.'

Joubert was a man with such reverence for old age that he didn't even publish anything until after his death. But the West hasn't valued old age since around the time that the Beatles just missed out on National Service. Now, being old means you don't recognise 'Poker Face' from the opening chords. Perhaps it is not old age that got small but old people. When I was a small child, old men had fought at Normandy and Dunkirk and Anzio. Now old men can only boast about taking drugs with Iggy Pop or Keith Richards or Pete Doherty. It's just not the same as landing on D-Day.

The generational divide in *Mad Men* is between those who have served – in World War Two, in Korea – and those who never served – the younger men, the sixties kids, the swingers and groovers of the coming age. Our immediate ancestors. For that's who we are – men who have never served – not God, not King, not country – we served nothing other than ourselves and our own desires.

And what does a man know of service who only room service knows?

The formerly young live their lives looking back at their salad niçoise days before their broad mind and narrow waist changed places.

But read your J.M. Barrie – rather than remembering the neutered Walt Disney vision in green tights – and you understand that the point is not that Peter Pan is forever youthful, but that he is incapable of growing up. He keeps his milk teeth forever. It is like Ronnie Wood and his silk scarves. They are not his glory but his tragedy. One hundred years on from the publication of *Peter and Wendy*, the boy who can never grow up is more relevant than ever.

Peter is ultimately a pathetic figure, the patron saint of the formerly young, hamstrung for all eternity on the edge of the adult world, clinging to the tattered rags of youth even as the world around him moves on and gets a bit bored with him, and can't really see the point of him. Even Wendy Darling turns away in the end.

When they met again Wendy was a married woman, and Peter was no more to her than a little dust in the box in which she had kept her toys. Wendy was grown up. You need not be sorry for her. She was one of the kind who likes to grow up.

And doesn't she sound exactly like one of your ex-girlfriends?

The great comfort blanket of the formerly young is football.

'Yeah, we played well in the second half.' No, you didn't – they did. They played well. Not you. Try getting Alex Ferguson or Arsène Wenger to pay your mortgage and see how far your 'we did this, we did that' gets you.

The all-consuming obsession with sport, when you see some football team as the epicentre of the universe – is the province of boys, not men. And of the formerly young.

Youth will always have certain things over age. There is nothing like knowing that you have time to burn. And no matter how sweet life gets later, you know that the one thing you will never have again is time to burn. For time is running out. It is always running out. But when you are young, it doesn't feel that way.

Yet when did callow youth become preferable to steely-eyed experience? Would we really prefer to be Vernon Kaye rather than George Clooney? A bit of grey can be quite attractive. Women love it. Or they pretend they do.

Being formerly young makes everything hard. Settling down with one woman. Being a parent. Dying. Having a bit of a dance. Being formerly young makes all of this tougher than it should be. But growing old – it could be good. Growing old – it could be liberating.

For the young know that they will never die – and they are wrong. And the old know that they are going to die – and they are right. What could be more liberating than that? What could be a greater incentive to enjoy every sandwich?

'I shall spend my pension on brandy and summer gloves and satin candles, and say we've no money for butter,' said Jenny Joseph, looking forward to a badly behaved dotage. 'I shall go out in my slippers in the rain and pick the flowers in other people's gardens and learn to spit.'

Sounds pretty good to me. Old age is not the same as death. It could be wild. It could be grand. Nobody cares any more. They stare straight through you. You can do what you like. Old age – love it, embrace it, bring it on.

Be a mad old man in a Fedora, clacking your dentures appreciatively as the girls go by in their summer dresses.

But are we really capable of it? Or will we be forever formerly young?

I don't remember my father ever being young. If he ever had a youth, then he lost it somewhere between leaving school at fourteen and fighting at Monte Cassino at nineteen. I was born at the right time. Where he was born into an age of depression, war and austerity, I lucked into an era of great music, infinite sexual opportunities and stupid haircuts.

Yet he grew up. In a way that I never did, in a way that I never could. Our years of peace and prosperity have ruined us for old age. If you fornicated in the mud of Woodstock, or saw The Jam in the Roxy, or watched the sun go down from Café del Mar, or caught the Stone Roses at Spike Island, then perhaps it is understandable.

Youth was so bloody good that old age is unwelcome, unbearable, unthinkable.

I often find myself haunting deserted record stores. Who would have thought that record stores would become old-fashioned, cob-webby places full of shuffling old men with jam sponge on their chins? A song came on that I loved. Something about a rude boy and his ability to get it up. Get it up and keep it there.

Oh, it was so good! I began to tap my feet. Then I looked at the two girls behind the counter.

'Who's this then?' I said.

They looked at each other with disbelief.

'Rihanna,' they said. *Duh.*

My wife quickly pulled me away.

'You didn't say it's got a good beat, did you?' she said.

No – but I did buy the record. Except nobody says record any more, do they?

Only the fifty million formerly young.

Our thirty-something coke taker – he is steeped in nostalgia. He pines for his golden years. But even as the blood was pumping through veins and brain he knew it was hopeless – you can't get back the time. Taking drugs when you are over twenty-five, it is like being a fat man in a Wayne Rooney shirt.

And so the formerly young charge on, boats against the current, wearing our replica football shirts and our thinning Liam Gallagher haircuts and our *Top Gear* 501s, borne back ceaselessly into the past, and always forgetting that Peter Pan is not lucky.

Peter Pan is cursed.

Twenty-Nine

Big World, Small Society

My son went to a state school and my daughter goes to a private school.

The girl is receiving an extraordinary education with great facilities in a stimulating environment that is giving her enough self-confidence to run the world. The boy was thrown into a seething maelstrom of depressed teachers, rioting kids and an environment where the very concept of education was widely despised.

My privately educated daughter is on the fast track to success – although she will probably end up punting down the river Cam with some bounder in a boater. My state-educated son emerged from his inner-city comprehensive with impressive A-levels in Knife Fighting, Crack Dealing and Intermediary GBH.

So we can see that both state and private schools have their good points.

No, they really do.

Anyone who goes to a state school learns that this is a

wicked world, red in tooth and claw, where dog eats dog and cat eats mouse. You come out of a state school with a PhD from the University of Life. Or at least the Polytechnic of Life.

But if you go to a private school, your young mind is opened up to all the glories of the world. You are helped at every step to fulfil your full potential. *You are not allowed to fail.* And if you are spared seeing this world in all its mediocrity and stupidity and horror and violence and venality – well, isn't that a good thing? Shouldn't every child in the world have an education like that?

These two schools do not merely represent different standards of education, but also different levels of aspiration. The children at this private school have great expectations while the children at this state school have no expectations. The two schools are four miles apart.

Oh, and several million light years.

And one thing is dead certain. If you send your child to a state school, then they will never be prime minister.

It has become a commonplace to say that we are now living in a post-meritocracy, where it is not what you can do that counts, but how much money your parents spent on your education.

The talk of a post-meritocracy began when David Cameron (Eton) and Nick Clegg (Westminster) were in the Rose Garden of 10 Downing Street, celebrating their coalition government. It was pointed out that while only 7 per cent of the population go to private schools, almost 70 per cent of the men and women around the Cabinet table were privately educated.

The Big Bang of the post-meritocracy is generally seen as the wonderful moment when David Cameron was reminded of his favourite political joke – Nick Clegg! – and, although he pretended to storm off in a huff, the leader of the Lib-Dems *truly did not care.*

That's what you get from a private education, some said. The ability to rise above it all. The talent to not give a damn. And – one wise voice muttered in my lughole – the judgement to gauge the true level of feeling behind any bit of banter.

It is true that the Rose Garden made Cameron and Clegg seem more alike than they ever had before. But the post-meritocracy really began with Tony Blair (Fettes).

When Blair told us about the importance of education, education, education, we had no idea that he was actually talking about private education, private education, private education.

Blair may have been a boarder at Fettes – motto: 'Success is all about not giving up' – but for most of the second half of the twentieth century, Britain had a prime minister who was educated by the state.

John Major went to Rutlish Grammar School in Merton Park, where he was caned. Maggie Thatcher went to Kesteven and Grantham Girls' School. Jim Callaghan went to a secondary school in Portsmouth, and started work at seventeen because he couldn't afford to go to university. Ted Heath went to a grammar school in Ramsgate. Harold Wilson was head boy at Wirral Grammar School for Boys.

Before Blair, you have to go all the way back to 16th October 1964 to find a privately educated prime minister: Old Etonian Alec Douglas-Home.

Stop and think about what a huge compliment that is to state education in the years after the war. From the time that Douglas-Home left office until Blair arrived in Downing Street there were five prime ministers over thirty-three years – and they were all educated in state grammar schools.

Much was made of Cameron being the nineteenth Old Etonian prime minister. But there was a gap of nearly fifty years between the eighteenth and nineteenth Old Etonian PM.

The golden age of meritocracy.

Long gone now.

It's true that Gordon Brown went to a state school in Kirkaldy, but then he never won an election, so I don't think he counts. And Brown is more than fifteen years older than Clegg and Cameron. These smooth sons of privilege are what our future looks like.

Cameron and Clegg are in those top jobs not just because their parents bought them a wonderful education but because there is no competition from their contemporaries who went to state schools. Someone once asked – Whatever happened to the British Picasso? And the answer was that the British Picasso probably died at the Somme, with so many of his generation.

And why did Clegg and Cameron only have to fight off an apocalyptically grumpy old Scot? Why wasn't Labour being led by an equally smooth, state-educated politician in his forties? Because that man, the unknown Labour leader, was educated at a comprehensive – a start in life right up there with dying in a ditch at the Somme.

And his name will be forever unknown.

Eton, Westminster, St Paul's, Highgate and Westminster are superior schools. But they were superior schools during those thirty-three years when every prime minister was educated by the state.

The great public schools of England were not in decline during those years of state-educated prime ministers. State schools were – for one brief shining moment – in the ascendant. It was an era when the children from ordinary homes were more than a match for the children of the rich. And what a national tragedy that those days of fairness and opportunity are gone.

When my son was studying Advanced Shoplifting at Islington Green Comprehensive Hellhole, those nice Blairs were our neighbours. But we did not clock them at too many school functions. Because they were bussing their kiddies to schools on the other side of town.

Labour politicians were the architects of the great comprehensive school disaster, but most of them would never have dreamed of sending their own children to a bog-standard inner-city comp. Tony Blair embodied the traditional Labour attitude to comprehensives – *I didn't go to one and I wouldn't send my child to one.* But you should. And so should your kids.

Anthony Crosland, Labour's Education Secretary in the sixties, set about the systematic destruction of the grammar schools with all the fervour of a Red Guard smashing priceless Ming vases. Crosland told his wife, 'I'm going to destroy every fucking grammar school.' And he did a pretty good job. Ninety per cent of the twelve hundred grammar schools that existed in the sixties have gone.

Crosland butchering the grammar schools really was the British equivalent of the Cultural Revolution in the People's Republic of China – an act of institutionalised vandalism done in the name of equality. Crosland, the archetype Bollinger Bolshevik, wanted to exterminate the grammar schools because they were elitist. In doing so, he laid the foundations for our post-meritocracy.

The grammar schools were the best mechanism for social mobility that this country ever had. The Labour Party burned that ladder and, terrified of seeming elitist, no subsequent government – Labour or Tory – has tried to restore it. Tory MP Graham Brady resigned from Shadow Cabinet specifically because Cameron would not support the 164 remaining grammar schools.

Our prime minister talks of the Big Society. But our educational apartheid ensures that we have exactly the opposite – a small society, a narrow society, a closed society.

Will we ever again have a prime minister who did not have a private education?

The fact that David Cameron went to Eton and Nick Clegg

went to Westminster says a lot about social mobility in our country today.

There isn't any.

Social mobility is dead now, and the evidence is sitting around the Cabinet table, and it is on the doorstep of Number 10 in the shape of our privately educated PM, and his privately educated deputy. If Clegg and Cameron had gone to a comprehensive school, you would never have heard of them.

And after all the jeering at Cameron for his Little Lord Fauntleroy background, it soon became clear that Clegg originates from exactly the same privileged strata of society. Should that bother us? Only because of what it says about opportunity in this country. If you want to get ahead, you need to get a private education. Private schools are now like the lifeboats on the *Titanic*.

Education is not the only mechanism to social mobility. But it is the greatest. And it is the most effective. And it is the most likely to propel the children of the working and middle class beyond the realm of their immediate surroundings. The solution is not tearing down private schools but elevating state schools.

Going to a private school doesn't make you a toff.

It makes you employable.

Does this educational apartheid matter?

Oh yes.

Never mind that it diminishes us all. Never mind about our

moral duty to make this country a fairer, more just place for everyone, no matter where they were born.

We need to change the blight of our educational apartheid for our own sakes. Because if it persists for generations, then this land will not be a comfortable or pleasant place to live for anyone.

Never underestimate the bitterness of those who are left at the bottom of the pile, with no way up or out. Do not dismiss them. One day you might wake up with one of them standing at the foot of your bed.

It isn't the 'poshness' of Cameron and Clegg that should trouble us.

It is the fact that our educational apartheid is now so deeply ingrained that these days a thick rich kid will always do better than a bright poor kid.

And that should break our hearts.

When I was young, they went to the moon.

I walked out into our back garden, wearing the uniform of my grammar school, and I watched the moon as the commentary from a hundred TV sets drifted out of open windows.

That's it, I thought. Now we will just keep on going.

But somehow we didn't.

My old grammar school is gone. They turned it into a comprehensive. David and Nick are in the Rose Garden of 10 Downing Street.

And nobody goes to the moon.